MW01146062

Let M

(A McClain Family Novella)

Alexandria House

Pink Cashmere Publishing, LLC
Arkansas, USA

Copyright © 2019 by Alexandria House
Cover image by Jaida A Photography

All rights reserved. This book or any portion thereof may not
be reproduced or used in any manner whatsoever without the
express written permission of the publisher except for the use
of brief quotations in a book review.

This is a work of fiction. Names, characters, businesses, places,
events and incidents are either the products of the author's
imagination or used in a fictitious manner. Any resemblance
to actual persons, living or dead, or actual events is purely
coincidental.

Printed in the United States of America

First Printing 2019

Pink Cashmere Publishing, LLC
pinkcashmerepub@gmail.com

Let Me Please You

She's the only sister in a family of alpha males. Loved, treasured, and sheltered by her brothers, Kat McClain is working to heal the pain of a failed marriage to a man she loved from her teenage years and move on with her life, but she's a woman, she has needs, and she is understandably lonely.

Tommy Kirby has protected her brother since he was barely a man and has been a silent staple in the McClain family for just as long. He loves his job and his life, is loyal to his employer, but more than anything, he wants a family of his own.

Perhaps these two are exactly what the other desires.

*** *This is a novella that takes place during the same time as* Let Me Show You, *book 3 of the McClain Brothers series.* ***

Prologue

Kathryn

"You're just gonna throw this away, throw *us* away? After all these years, the life we've built? That's it? It's over?" Wayne's voice was weak, shaky. He sounded hurt, like he was innocent. As if I was the one who'd stepped outside the marriage, repeatedly. Like *I* was the cheater.

"No, Wayne. You threw this, *us*, away when you lost control of your little penis. You threw our marriage away in receptacles named Shan and Felicity—oh! And let's not forget Carmen. What was I supposed to do? Let you dog me out forever?"

"I didn't dog you out. At least not on purpose. I...you know I got a problem. I'm in counseling for it!"

"Yes, Wayne. I know you are. You're in counseling with *Carmen*, the same Carmen you're fucking. You are fucking your counselor, remember?"

"Now that was an accident. I told you that!"

"Does she know about whatever trick gave you chlamydia? She better get checked out."

No reply from my hoe-ass husband.

Then a thought hit me. "Carmen burned you?! She's the one who gave you that shit?!"

"Uh..."

"Wooooow!"

"Kat, listen—"

"Nope. Sign the papers. Release me from this supposed marriage."

"I can't."

"You better."

"I'ma contest it."

"For what? I'm giving you everything—the cars, the house, the furniture. Shit, I'm even giving you the damn cat!"

"I bought Milky, anyway," he muttered.

"And I don't like Milky's ass. Look, the only thing I'm keeping is my business, and if you try to take that from me, I will wrestle it from your cold, dead hands. And I mean *dead hands.*"

"I wouldn't take your business from you, baby. I love you too much for that."

And that's when I hung up, because…*screw that.* Love? I couldn't believe he'd fixed his mouth to say that word after the shit he put me—matter of fact…

I decided to send him a text: *Use your fake love to sign those damn papers. And don't call me again. EVER.*

Asshole: *I wish you'd give us another chance. Please, baby.*

Me: *Hell. No.*

1

Kathryn

I loved living in St. Louis. Loved being around my little brother. Was in heaven being around my nephew all the time, because he was beautiful and sweet, just like his daddy. Being around Little Leland reminded me of when I was a girl, a five-year-old who had been the youngest until his father was born. I was in awe of my baby brother when he entered this world, felt like he was *my* baby. Sometimes, I felt the same way about his son. Especially since I would probably never have a child of my own.

That wasn't by choice. Well, not at first. When Wayne and I first married, right after we graduated from college, we were too busy working on our futures to have a baby. Me, building what was now a thriving online boutique, and him, jumping from one ill-fated business to another, never really finding his footing. His latest venture, selling life insurance, wasn't fairing any better for him. Later, when I realized the cheating that started in high school and kept popping up throughout our marriage was never going to stop, I crossed having kids off my list. I wasn't going to bring a child into that mess. What I wished more than anything, though, was that I'd had the common sense sooner to get myself out of said mess. I was just so…dumb and loyal.

Too loyal.

Too understanding.

Too damn stupid.

But I figured things out, finally saw my life for what it was, what it had been, a colossal waste of time and energy and love.

Yeah, I poured my love down the drain, dumped it in a

trash can, threw it on the ground and stomped on it. And now, it was gone. I had no more to give to anyone but my family, especially my Little Leland.

Anyway, despite all that, I loved my life, but I hated waiting. I'd exhausted my patience with grown folks, so sitting in this gorgeous living room waiting for Leland to decide to stop screwing Kim and come conduct this meeting with me so that I could…shit, what did I have to do with my life other than work on my boutique, *Quintessence*, the only baby I'd ever birthed?

Damn, my life was pathetic.

I was thirty-three years old and alone and admittedly horny with no social life that didn't involve my family. Yeah, I had friends back in LA, a few old ones in Texas, but they were all a part of my life with Wayne, and I was trying to distance myself from him by any means necessary. Plus, I couldn't deal with the pitied looks or genuine sympathy from them regarding the tragic ending of what most people on the outside looking in considered to be a solid union, an unbreakable bond. You know, soul mate shit.

Yeah, I once thought that, too.

But then there was Shan and Felicity and fucking Carmen—just to name a few.

That son-of-a—

"Kit-Kaaaaat! You been waiting long?" Leland bellowed, as he *finally* bounded his big ass into the living room and plopped down on the sofa sitting opposite the loveseat I had planted my wide ass on.

"You *think* I've been waiting long? I mean, you texted me at the break of dawn, said we needed to meet at nine this morning. It is now ten, my coffee cup is empty, and so is my level of patience. This meeting better be important."

He gave me a silly-ass grin. "Damn, you woke up on the wrong side of my old bed or something?"

I rolled my eyes. "I replaced the bed in your condo when I moved in, remember? I wasn't going to be sleeping where you and Kim got freaky. That's nasty as hell!"

"You walk on the carpet? Use the shower? Eat at the counter? If so, I hate to tell you—"

"Shut your nasty ass up. What did you want to meet about?"

"Mean ass...I need you to get with Tommy to coordinate an official security schedule. I don't want Kim and the baby uncovered at any time. That even means when you're keeping him. So, maybe y'all can assign certain team members to certain people or rotate them or whatever. I would say you need someone assigned to you, too, but I know your ass ain't going for that."

"And you'd be right. I do not need a bodyguard."

"Whatever. Anyway, there's that, and Kim's birthday is coming up, so I need you to help me put together a party for her. Then, put together a list of vacation destinations for this summer. Oh, and Kim's planning a dinner party. Not sure when it's supposed to be, but you're invited."

As I scribbled on my notepad, I nodded without looking up. "I know. She called and invited me already."

"Oh, yeah...I forgot y'all be talking to each other behind my back. Y'all better not be talking about me."

"We always discuss how young and stupid you are." I looked up to see a frown on my baby brother's face and laughed. "I'm just playing with you, Leland Randall."

"Play too damn much. Anyways, that's it."

"Good, because that's enough."

"Like I don't pay you well."

"You sure do, little brother. You bought these shoes."

As I wiggled my Jimmy Choo-covered feet in the air, he shook his head.

TOMÁS

"Mamá! Where you been? Why you ain't been answering your phone?" I asked, rolling over in my bed.

"Toe-mee? Ju been calling me? I see no call from ju, mijo. How ju doing?" my mom replied.

I smiled. My mom's voice, her accent, always reminded me of home and my childhood. Good times and good memories. "I called *and* texted. Tryna make sure you got that money I sent."

"I got it. Ju send too much, mijo! Ju got enough to buy food for juself? How is ju sugar?"

I sighed. "It's fine. I'm fine. I get paid a lot. I got plenty left for myself. Just wanna make sure you and Josefina and the baby are taken care of."

"We are! Still got money left from last month. I tell ju…ju send too much. Too much! Ju work today?"

"Yeah, gotta get up and head out soon."

"Okay. Ju be careful. Tell Big West I say hi!"

Chuckling, I said, "Okay," without correcting South's name or reminding her that I was working for Leland now. It didn't matter anyway.

After we ended the call, I sat up and stared at myself in the dresser mirror, thinking about how I thought I'd be married with a kid by now. Hell, that's what I really wanted. To settle down. But my last relationship—with Bridgette—didn't work out. No hard feelings there at all, though. It just wasn't meant to be, and it's not like she didn't tell me from jump she wasn't the white-picket-fence, baby-in-a-carriage type. So it wasn't like I could be mad at her even if I wanted to.

I just…I was tired of being single. Watching South fall in love didn't help the situation, and now I was around the baby McClain brother who was so crazy about his wife, the shit was insane.

Yeah, I was a big nigga—six-nine to be exact. Three hundred pounds. No flab. I kept in shape, had to in my line of work. I was a professional protector. A big intimidating dark-skinned motherfucker, and I knew it. But shit, big niggas need love, too.

*****

A trick of my trade that I'd learned a long time ago was to be seen but remain silent. I stood guard, shielded my clients, absorbed their surroundings, and stayed alert. Kind of like lethal furniture. Always there if I was needed, but not flashy with it. South hired me when I was nineteen and he was almost thirty. Dude was a good employer, loyal than a motherfucker, and was still paying me even though I was protecting his brother now instead of him. I missed LA, but I needed the change this move to St. Louis provided, and Leland was a cool boss. He and his sister kept me rolling, arguing all the time, but it was easy to see that dynamic was just a part of their love for one another. And Kat was nice to look at, always had been, despite her being forbidden fruit since I was on her brother's payroll and I knew for a fact how protective South was of her. I wasn't trying to mess up my six-figure salary, not that she'd want to fuck my bodyguard ass anyway. But still…

Back to the whole bodyguard invisibility thing. Sometimes it worked against me, because from the moment I arrived in Leland's living room and sat down across from Kat, she didn't lift her head or acknowledge me. So, after ten minutes, I cleared my throat, and her head popped up.

"Shit! When did you get here?" she shrieked.

"Uh, about ten minutes ago?"

"Damn, you're like a ghost."

I frowned slightly. "Okay…"

"Well, anyway, Leland wanted us to meet so we can come

up with a security team schedule. Did he tell you?"

"Yeah. I was thinking about assigning Kole to you when you have the baby, Quezz to Kim and the baby when she has him, and I'll handle Leland. Me and Kole can do the whole family, or all three of us if the situation calls for it."

She twisted her mouth to the side. She had some nice lips and almost always wore dark lipstick. Yeah, I noticed shit like that about her. And how she usually wore her thick hair in a ponytail, how smooth her skin was. She looked so damn much like Leland, but in a feminine way. Kat was fucking beautiful. And I'm not saying that just because I was horny as hell and she was the only single woman I was around a lot. Or at least I guessed she was single.

I'd always thought she was attractive. Tall and stacked like a full deck of spades.

"Why you assigning Kole to me?" she asked.

"Uh, I don't know. You don't like Kole?"

"I don't know Kole. I know *you*."

"Yeah, but I got the most experience. I should be looking out for Leland."

"Because he's the basketball star?"

"Well, yeah."

"So fuck the little sister, huh? I'm the one who always has his baby and the baby needs the best security. Kole be too busy looking at random women's asses to protect a damn flea."

She wasn't lying about that. I'd had to get onto Kole about that shit before. I was a second from firing his ass since Leland had given me that authority.

"Uh, let me run this by Leland, then. See if he's okay with me shadowing you and the baby instead of him."

"No, he said *we* were supposed to make the schedule. I say, you with me and the baby. Quezz with Kim and the baby when she has him, and Kole with Leland. Or…fire Kole's ass and hire someone with some sense."

She crossed her legs, her tight black skirt rose up her thighs a little, and all I could say was, "Okay."

2

Kathryn

So here's the thing: I was horny as hell.

What my cheating husband had been lacking in inches, he more than made up for in nastiness, and although I wouldn't touch his chlamydic dick with a horse's pussy, I missed having regular sex. But I had no prospects, and I was tired of playing with myself. There was only so far porn and a vivid imagination could take a girl. That was one of the reasons I spent so much time with Little Leland. Besides the fact that I loved him to death, he kept my mind occupied and off my vacant vagina.

I kissed his little cheek and nuzzled his baby-smelling neck and sighed. Then I lifted my eyes to Tommy, who was staring at his phone. He had to be the quietest giant I'd ever met. And the giantest one, too. I was six-two, and there were only a few men I knew who dwarfed me, including my oldest and youngest brothers. But damn, I felt short as hell around him, and he was kind of cute, too, in a rugged way—always a serious expression on his face. Tommy looked…*mean*, like he'd fuck something up on a dime. *I bet he can screw like a damn Tasmanian devil. Got those big hands…*

What was wrong with me? I couldn't be *that* horny. Damn!

"You texting Bridgette?" I asked, making his head pop up in surprise.

"What? No," he said, leaning back on the loveseat.

"Oh. How is she? I haven't seen her in a while, but I always like being around her. She's funny."

He shrugged. "We don't talk, so I don't know."

"Oh? You two broke up?"

"Yep."

"Do you ever eat?"

That ever-present frown of his deepened. "Eat? Yeah. I ain't this big for nothing."

"I never see you eat."

"Because I'm on the job when you see me. I don't eat on the job."

"But I've seen you follow Ev and Leland around for entire days. When do you eat?"

"When I can."

"Damn, that's dedication."

He shrugged.

"You always been so quiet?"

"You always been so nosy?"

My mouth fell open. I didn't know he could be so, I don't know, sassy. Can a man be sassy? "You're sitting up in my house not talking. It's weird."

"I'm protecting you and the baby. I talk when it involves protecting you and the baby."

"First of all, you're protecting the baby, not me, because I don't need protecting. And I can't deal with the silence, so you gon' talk to me."

"Talking is distracting. I need to be alert and aware."

"Of what? We're locked up inside my condo. Who gon' fuck with us in here anyway? Leland is doing the most."

"No, he's being smart."

"How much does Ev pay you?"

"How much does Leland pay *you*?"

"Damn, you getting real smart-assed up in here. So you *do* have a personality? All these years of seeing you stand around my brother and I didn't know that."

"Anybody ever tell you that you talk a lot?"

"You do know I'm your boss right now, right? And you're gonna talk to me like that?"

"Did I lie?"

"Where are you from?"

"Originally? Brownsville."

"Texas?"

"Yep."

"Where'd you meet Ev?"

"Miami."

"How?"

He shook his head. "You're not gonna stop, are you?"

"Nope."

He sighed. "At a strip club. I was a bouncer. He came there, saw me, and asked if I wanted to work for him. Offered me more money than I ever thought I could make as a bodyguard, so I said yeah. It didn't hurt that I was a fan of his."

"You liked working for him?"

"Yeah, South is a good dude."

"You like working for Leland?"

"Yeah, he's cool."

I was about to ask another question when my phone began to ring.

Wayne.

The same Wayne who still had not signed the divorce papers.

Standing from the sofa, I handed Little Leland to a bewildered-looking Tommy. "Watch him for a minute. I'll be right back."

Before he could protest — because he looked petrified — I rushed to my bedroom, closed the door, and answered my phone with, "Sign the fucking papers, nigga!"

"Kat—"

"It's been more than a year since we split! I need to move on! Sign them!"

"I will if you have dinner with me. Have one last dinner with me and I'll sign the papers at the table."

I hung the phone up, because I didn't have time to play with his childish ass. And when I returned to my living room, I retrieved my nephew and reclaimed my seat on the sofa. Feeling Tommy's eyes on me, I growled, "What?!"

"Uh, nothing," he said, with raised eyebrows. Then he

returned his attention to his phone.

TOMÁS

"Si, si. Esta bien. No, eso functionará. Gracias, tio." I ended the call, dropped my phone in my lap, and looked up to find Kat's eyes on me. In response, I lifted my eyebrows, and said, "What?"

"You know Spanish?" she asked.

"Yeah. Is that a problem, Ms. McClain?"

"No, but you know *Spanish* Spanish. Not struggle, I-took-a-class-in-high-school-but-didn't-learn-shit Spanish."

I shrugged. "It's really my first language. My mom's Mexican."

Her jaw dropped. "You're half Mexican? With a name like Tommy?"

"Tomás."

"You don't look half nothing but negro."

"She's Afro-Mexican. There are black people in Mexico, you know?"

"Woooow. So you can just bust out with Spanish at any moment? Say something else."

"What?"

"Speak Spanish again."

"Okay…" I thought for a minute. "Hablas denasiado. Es un problema."

"You're talking shit about me, aren't you?"

"Why would you think that?"

"Because you're smirking at me. You need to be nicer to me, *Tomás*. I'll get your ass fired."

I tilted my head to the side. "Are you like this because you're the only sister?"

She frowned. "Like what?"

"Mean and bossy and nosy and loquacious."

Her eyebrows tented, and for once, she didn't reply.

"Yeah, I know what that word means. I can read *and* write, Ms. McClain."

Her eyelashes fluttered. Damn, she was pretty. "I never said you couldn't."

"But your reaction tells me you thought I was unintelligent."

"No, I just…I haven't heard you say much else besides 'boss man' in like ten years."

"Because talking is a distraction. Remember?"

"You want me to shut up?"

"This is your house. I can't tell you what to do with your mouth, Ms. McClain."

Her eyes widened before she dropped them and licked her lips. "What did you say about me in Spanish?"

"You talk too much. It's a problem."

She rolled her eyes. "Just tell me what you said, negro. I mean, *Mexi*-negro."

I chuckled. "That *was* what I said."

"So you really think I talk too much, huh, *Tomás*?"

"Yes."

She adjusted Little Leland — the reason I was sitting in her living room — on her lap. "Then I'll just shut up, since that's what you want."

"Like I said, I can't tell you what to do with your mouth, Ms. McClain. You can keep it open or close it. It's up to you."

She gave me a strange look before focusing her attention on the baby.

3

Kathryn

It was my merciful off-day from being Leland's assistant, so I was doing *Quintessence* work, trying to forget that I woke up hunching the air. Shit, I was so tuned up that a strong wind could make my clit jump through my clothes. Fucking Wayne. If he hadn't cheated on me, given me chlamydia, and broken my heart, he could be eating my box right now! So fucking selfish.

I sighed and closed my eyes, shutting out my computer screen. This was not what my life was supposed to look like. Being sexless sucked.

Grabbing my phone, I scrolled through my Instagram feed, smiling at the pictures my friends and family had shared. I rolled my eyes at a picture *Tea Steepers* posted of Leland and Kim leaving the Cyclones stadium and wondered why I was following that silly-ass blog. I mean, the caption of the picture was: *Leland "fine as hell" McClain and his cougar wife are still going strong.*

Stupid as hell.

I was about to scroll past the picture when I noticed the man standing behind them.

Tommy.

Tomás.

Damn, he was fine. Big and fine and surprisingly witty. With a nice deep voice. Good teeth. Thick hair. Tattoos.

I rubbed the back of my neck and licked my lips, wondered who was enjoying the feel of his big hands and then snapped out of whatever sexless lust fog I'd wandered into.

Then I sighed, stood from my sofa, and headed to my bedroom and my damn dildo.

Fuck my life.

TOMÁS

"You got any friends?" she asked.

With my eyes still on my phone, I said, "Yeah, a few."

"You ever spend time with them? All I see you do is work. You work like all the time."

"We keep in touch, but no…I don't go out much, and I like working all the time. I got a good job."

"I guess…you ever been married?"

I looked up from my phone and gave her my attention. "No."

"Why?"

"I don't know. Haven't found my wife yet."

"Got any kids?"

"No."

"Siblings?"

"Yes. A sister. Josefina."

"Damn, you really *are* Mexican! What's your last name?"

"Kirby."

"Tomás Kirby? Kirby isn't a Hispanic name, is it?"

"No."

She sat there giving me a confused look. "So, you're *not* Mexican?"

"My father wasn't. He was African American."

"Oh! Was? He passed away?"

"Uh-huh. When I was a teenager."

"Sorry. I know how that is. What's your middle name?"

"What's yours?"

"Ann."

"That's nice."

"You gonna tell me yours?"

"No."

"Why?"

"Because I don't wanna hear you talking shit about it."

She smiled. "It's that bad?"

"You'll never know."

Her phone buzzed and she checked the screen, typed something — I guess a text message — then laid her phone down and kind of stared into space. No more questions.

Since Little Leland was down for a nap, it was super quiet, uncomfortably quiet, so I said, "That's all it takes, huh?"

With a furrowed brow, she looked up at me. "What?"

"You hear a phone buzz and you stop talking? Is that like the camera flash in *Get Out*?"

She gave me a smirk. "So you got jokes, *Tomássss*?"

"You really like my government name, don't you?"

"Uh-huh. I like your middle name, too. What was it again?"

"Nice try."

"Whatever. And phones buzzing don't shut me up. Messages from my ex do."

"He ain't scared to text you? I would be."

"Why?"

"Because you kicked his ass!"

"How you know that?! You weren't even there when it happened, were you?"

"I overheard South talking about it."

"Ooooh, so you're an eavesdropper."

"No, but if I'm in a car driving him somewhere, I can't help what I hear. I hear a lot of stuff."

"Like what?"

"Can't tell you."

"Now you wanna be close-lipped but you can spread *my* business?"

"Uh, I said it to you, so who am I spreading it to?"

"That's not the point. The point is —" Her phone buzzed

again, to which she hissed, "This motherfucker just will not quit." She looked up from the phone, glued her eyes to me, and asked, "Why do men cheat?"

I blinked and frowned a little. "Uh, I don't know."

"When you cheated on whoever, why did you do it?"

"Who said I ever cheated on anyone?"

"Did you...or have you?"

"Uh..."

"Uh, *what*?"

"Isn't this a conversation you should be having with one of your brothers?"

"No. They'll just start talking about how they're gonna kick Wayne's ass or how they should've killed him a long time ago. They won't talk to me about relationship stuff, because I'm their sister and it weirds them out."

"I can see that. I'm not trying to talk to my sister about that stuff, either."

"So tell me. Why?"

I sighed and adjusted myself on the loveseat. "In my case, I was young, stupid, didn't take the relationship serious. I don't know."

"Why would a husband cheat on his wife, a wife he claims to love?"

"Well, I've never been a husband, never really been in love, but I believe if you love someone, you don't disrespect or hurt or embarrass them. I would make it my business to protect the heart of the woman I loved."

She stared at me and dropped her eyes, a rare move for her. "My husband—he's still my husband, unfortunately. He...I think he loved me at first, but I think he stopped at some point. He had to. That's the only way he could've kept cheating on me."

"Do you...still love him?" I asked, and for some reason, I really wanted to hear the answer.

Her eyes met mine and she bit her bottom lip, rubbed her hands over the thighs of the jeans she wore. "No. I think I fell out of love with him a few hoes ago. I just…I got with him in high school, and we were together for so long. I think forgiving him and staying with him just became a habit."

"Until it didn't?"

She sighed. "Yeah, until it didn't."

4

Kathryn

"I think he likes you," I said, as I returned to my living room with a glass of water for Tommy and a bowl of cut-up mango for me and my baby boy.

Smiling at Little Leland, who was perched in his lap giggling at him, he replied, "Yeah, I guess he had to learn to like me since you stay handing him to me."

Taking the baby from him, I said, "Well, you're here anyway, so why take him to the bathroom or kitchen with me when I don't have to?"

He pulled a bottle out of his pocket and opened it. I stared at him as he popped a pill in his mouth and washed it down with some of the water. Placing the bottle back in his pocket, he looked up at me. "What?"

"What you taking? Tylenol? You tryna act like I'm giving you a headache or something?" I quipped.

"No, not today. I mean, you *can* give a dude a headache, though..."

I rolled my eyes. "Well, what was it?"

"Why is it your business?" he asked, adjusting on the loveseat, stretching his impossibly long legs out before him.

"It's my business because this is my home and I need to know if you're taking crack or something around my nephew."

"You don't take crack, Ms. McClain. You smoke it."

"See how you knew that and I didn't?"

He shook his head. "Wow."

"Are you gonna tell me what it was?"

He sighed. "It was Metformin."

I frowned. "Met who?"

"*Metformin*. I take it to control my blood sugar. I'm a diabetic."

"What?!" I yelled, startling Little Leland who I then tightly hugged and kissed. "You're a diabetic? But...how?"

"Uh, genetics? My mom's a diabetic."

"But...you never eat. I never see you eat. I offer you food and you never take it, and shouldn't you be taking that pill with food or something?"

"I do eat, Ms. McClain; you just never see me eat, and I was supposed to take my pill when I woke up this morning, with my breakfast. I forgot, so I took it when I remembered."

"Oh...you feel okay? I mean, are you all right?"

"I'm fine. Been on this medicine since I was like twenty-three. My blood sugar is under control."

"You sure?"

"Yeah, I'm positive, Ms. McClain."

"You want some mangoes? They're good," I said, as I popped a piece in my mouth.

He licked his lips, looked me up and down, and said, "I bet they are, but no thanks."

We stared at each other for a minute or so, and then he turned his attention to his phone, and I turned mine to my nephew and our snack.

*****

"Skip you, skip you, reverse back to me, reverse back to me, draw four, Uno, Uno out! I wooooon! I wooooon! Damn, how you gon' be Mexican and lose an Uno game?" I asked, as I hopped up from my kitchen table and shook my booty. Little Leland giggled in his high chair as he messily ate his French fries.

"That's so damn racist. You know that?" Tommy said, shaking his head.

"Whatever. Your deal, since you lost...*again*."

"Naw, I'm through playing this game with your cheating ass. How you gonna have a hand full of wild cards and a damn blue five?"

"Luck of the draw, Tomás. And how did I cheat when you dealt?"

"That's what I'm tryna find out. You're diabolical."

"There you go with those *Universidad* words of yours. Give me another one, Señor Kirby."

"In Spanish or English?"

"English. You be sneak dissing me in Spanish."

He chuckled. "Okay. Did you know you are very...specious?"

I grabbed my phone. "Spell it."

"I'll save you the trouble. It means deceptive, like how you deceptively cheated during that Uno game."

I gave him a smirk. "You're just an unskilled Uno player and a sore loser."

"I bet I'd kill you at checkers, though."

"We'll never know."

"Why?"

"Because I don't know how to play checkers."

"I could teach you, Ms. McClain. Or are you scared of losing?"

"I'm not scared of losing, I just don't like losing. I've had more than enough experience with that."

Damn, there went my good mood. I blinked back tears and turned my attention to my little ray of sunshine. "Come on, baby boy. I bet you need to be changed."

As I lifted Little Leland from the high chair and left the kitchen, I could feel Tommy's sympathetic eyes on my back.

TOMÁS

"Damn...you beat me," I muttered, genuinely surprised she'd caught on to checkers so fast.

"I did?!" she squeaked.

"Yeah...you captured all my pieces. Ain't that some shit?"

She grinned, then frowned. "You let me win?"

I shook my head. "The way you get on my nerves? Hell no! You're a quick learner and a natural strategist. I guess most specious people are, though."

She rolled her eyes.

"Anyway, you won fair and square. Good job, Ms. McClain."

Her smile reappeared. "Thank you!"

"You're welcome. You really like winning, don't you?"

"Who doesn't? Don't you like winning?"

I shrugged. "I don't like competing at all."

"For real?"

"Yeah, is that so hard to believe? I don't like competing. With anyone. In anything. I mean, these games are fun, but losing at them won't make me lose any sleep. And as far as my career or business? I like doing my best at what I do. I take pride in anything I do, but I ain't messed up about what the next man is doing. It's not my concern."

"What about in relationships? You like competition in your relationships?"

"What kind of question is that? Who the hell likes competition in a relationship?"

She did a little one-shoulder shrug.

I leaned forward and looked her in the eye. "If I'm with a woman, I quickly show her there ain't no competition when it comes to what I got for her, what I *give* to her."

"So you've never been cheated on?"

I shook my head. "Nope. I don't tolerate it."

"But you've cheated."

"Like I said, I was stupid."

"But you're not stupid anymore?"

"Do you think I'm stupid?"

"Not at all, Tomás."

"And since cheating is also stupid, that would mean a cheating woman would be a stupid woman. I'm not attracted to stupid women."

"What kind of women are you attracted to, Tomás?" she asked, lifting an eyebrow.

"Hmm, assertive, strong, attractive...*loquacious* women."

"Really, now?"

I gave her a smile and nodded, was about to add specious to my list when Little Leland started crying. Him waking up from his nap had kept my ass from crossing a line I had no business even being near.

5

Kathryn

It had been a bad day, one of those days when I didn't keep my nephew, didn't do any work, and had nothing but time to fill my head with thoughts I should have been pushing away. Thoughts of the past — past smiles, past love, past passion with the man who took my virginity and my heart. Past foolishness like me being faithful to him while he hopscotched around, slinging his peen from sea to shining sea. Past affairs, past heartaches, past forgiveness, past fights, past reconciliations. Then I started thinking about my mama. My sweet, sweet mama, wishing I could hug her, let her wrap her meaty arms around me, hear her tell me it would all be all right, because it didn't feel like it would ever be all right.

Being hurt by someone you love is fucked up. *Really* fucked up.

The only reason I'd made the effort to dress up, put on makeup, and get my hair done was because this was Kim's party and she'd invited me and we'd grown close. I had my doubts about her when she and Leland first got together but had now spent enough time with her to know she adored my little brother and meant him no harm. So she was my friend now, and friends don't let friends down. But sitting at that table with her and Leland and Leland's friend Polo, his girl Kendra, Kim's cousin Zabrina and her man, along with Cyclones' center Drayveon Walker, I felt out of place and uncomfortable. Partially because of all the damn happy couples at the table, and partially because I knew Kim was trying to fix me up with this young-ass center, as she knew I was lonely as hell. Shit, I was an inch from being depressed. But I wasn't in the mood to get to know a new man when I spent years thinking I knew my husband.

So before dessert was served, I excused myself to the bathroom, stayed in there an inappropriate amount of time, and when I emerged, announced that I was leaving because I wasn't feeling well.

"A'ight," Leland said. "Aye, Tommy!"

"Why are you calling Tommy?" I asked.

"So he can drive you home since you don't feel well."

"I can drive myself, Leland."

"No, you can't. Stop tryna be tough."

"What about my car?"

"I'll make sure it gets to you."

Sitting in the back of my brother's SUV, I stared out the window as a characteristically quiet Tommy navigated the streets of the community outside St. Louis where Leland's mansion was, into the city that I'd grown to love. The radio was on SiriusXM's Heart and Soul station, the music transitioning from Queen Naija's *Medicine* to Musiq Soulchild's *Dontchange*.

Our song.

Fuck.

I closed my eyes, sighed, and said, "Can you change the station?"

Tommy lowered the volume on the radio. "What?"

Tears had filled my eyes and were snaking their way down my face as I repeated myself. "C-can you change the station?"

He turned the radio off. Didn't say a word until he'd parked in front of my building and opened the back passenger-side door for me. "Um...let me help you out."

Wiping my face, I took his proffered hand, climbed out of the vehicle, and muttered, "Thank you," started walking toward the building, and stopped when I heard Tommy shout, "Wait!"

Turning around, I watched him trot toward me, my clutch in his hand. Damn, I was really messed up in the head.

"You forgot this," he said, his baritone voice soft, sympathetic.

"Yeah, I did," I agreed, taking the purse from him and swiping at the damn tears that decided to make another appearance in front of this man.

"Come on. Let me walk you to your door."

All I could do was nod as his big hand wrapped around my upper arm and let him usher me inside the building. At my door, he asked for my key, unlocked the door, and once I'd walked inside, asked, "You gonna be all right?"

I scoffed, "Does it look like I am?"

"You need me to stay?"

I shook my head. "No. If you stay, Leland will think something is wrong."

"Something *is* wrong."

"Yeah, but nothing that'll be fixed by you staying here. Goodnight, Tommy," I said. Then I stood there and stared into his dark, compassionate eyes.

He scratched his eyebrow and the wiry hair covering his chin. "If you're sure. Goodnight, Ms. McClain."

Turning his wide back to me, he began to walk away, his ass looking delicious in his jeans, remnants of his cologne crowding the air outside my door.

"Tommy, wait!"

Spinning on his heels, he was back in my face in seconds, his big body towering over mine. "You need something?"

Placing a hand on his hard chest, I said, "Yeah. You."

TOMÁS

She clutched my black t-shirt, pulled on it until my face was inches from hers, and then pressed her soft lips against mine. When she backed away a little, her teary eyes had narrowed.

"M-Ms—" I stuttered, only to be cut off by her.

"I do want you to stay."

"Uh, okay. But we can't—"

"I want you to stay with me in my bed. I want *you.*"

"I can't do—"

Her lips were on mine again, her hands dropping from my chest as she licked my lips, and I opened my mouth for her, because shit, what else was I supposed to do? But when her hand cupped my crotch where my dick was already hard as hell, I jumped back, and yelled, "What are you doing?!"

"Tryna fuck you!" she replied.

I shook my head. "We can't do that and you know we can't."

"Because you don't want to? You don't think I'm attractive?" she asked, her brow a network of creases.

"No, I mean, yes…I think you're very attractive, but I work for your brother. Hell, I work for *two* of your brothers."

"Did you sign a contract promising not to screw me or something?"

"No, but I ain't tryna get fired. South trusts me. Leland, too."

"They trust you to guard bodies, correct? Well, right now, I need you to guard mine. Especially my pus—"

"Ms. McClain—"

"Kat! Or Kathryn!"

"I'm not doing this."

"You scared?"

"Yeah, scared of losing my damn job, and you're still married anyway."

"Not by choice! The motherfucker won't sign the papers!"

Her neighbor's door opened, and he peeped his head out, fixing his eyes on us. We *were* loud as hell, so I backed her into the condo and closed the door behind me. "Look—"

She yanked her dress over her head and dropped her

panties and I swear my dick tried to bust through the zipper of my pants.

When she unfastened and dropped her bra and all her thickness was on display, I growled, "Fuck it," and pounced on her, kissing her, rubbing her round ass, closing my eyes as she moaned into my mouth.

I felt her fumbling with my jeans. "I got it," I said, after I ended our kiss, and a few seconds later, I was naked, too.

She stared at my dick, then lifted her eyes to my face. "Uh..."

"You changed your mind?" I asked. "It's okay if—"

She stuck her tongue down my throat as she backed me up to her couch, giving me no choice but to sit on it, then she straddled my lap, still kissing me. She grabbed my dick, and I managed to reclaim my mouth. "Hold up," I said, lifting her from my lap. I left the couch and dug my wallet out of my jeans, dug a condom out of my wallet, and as I covered myself, I said, "You don't make sure your man has one of these?"

She licked her lips, her eyes glued below my waist. "I've only ever been with one man. We were married, so we didn't use them, but we should've. I just didn't think about one of those."

I froze. "You've only been with him? Ever?"

"Yeah."

"Then I can't do this."

"Why not?! I'm hot and wet and horny! Shit, come on, Tomás!"

"It ain't right, Ms—Kathryn. It—"

She turned around on the sofa, got on her knees, poked her ass out, and hell, my feet just started moving on their own, and the next thing I knew, I had slid two fingers into her wetness. Damn, she was hot as hell. And wet as hell. She definitely didn't lie about that.

"Oh!" she whined.

I played with her for a minute or two, smiled at the sounds

she made and the way she wiggled that gorgeous ass at me, and then wet the head of my shaft with her juices before sliding, or trying to slide, it inside her. Shit! She was tighter than a motherfucker!

"Uh!" she whimpered.

"Relax, baby," I said. "Let me in."

"I'm trying to," she moaned.

"Wanna stop?"

"No! Put it in!"

"You're so tight…"

I worked my dick in slowly, finally making my way inside her, eased out, and plunged back in, causing her to scream and collapse against the back of the couch. Grabbing her hips, I thrusted in and out, closed my eyes, and groaned at her snugness as her moans and cries filled my ears like a symphony.

"You feel so good, baby. Damn!" I mumbled. "Shit!"

"Oh! Oh! Oh!" she answered.

I slid my hand up her back and back down to grip her ass cheek, gliding in and out of her until she began to jerk, her pussy contracting around me, and then I filled that damn condom, my whole body tensing up as I screamed her name.

Kathryn

"I need to go." His voice was so soft and gentle, such a contrast to his size and the way he'd man-handled my coochie earlier.

I peeled my eyes open and nodded against his chest. "Okay."

"Uh…you all right?" he asked, as I lifted from his body and he stood from the couch.

"I'm better than all right."

He smiled as he pulled his clothes on, leaned over and kissed me, then said, "Good."

After he left, I looked down at my body, which didn't even feel like it belonged to me anymore, and said, "Damn."

6

TOMÁS

After I dropped the boss's car off early that morning, I went home to my apartment and crashed. Woke up realizing it was my day off and flipped over in the bed, deciding I'd fully catch up on my sleep. When I finally climbed out of bed, it hit me. I mean, the truth that I'd had sex with Kathryn McClain crashed into me head-on. Not that I had forgotten how she smelled and felt, how good every moment of that was to me, but something about being wide awake, the sun at its peak in the sky, made it more…real.

What in the whole fuck had I done? South trusted me. Yeah. I was technically working for Leland now, but South still signed my checks, had been since he took a chance on me ten years ago, and I screwed his baby sister knowing he was protective of her? So was Leland and the damn twins, too.

Shit.

I fucked up.

Standing over the toilet emptying my bladder, I closed my eyes and shook my head. What was I going to do? How was I supposed to fix this? Shit, how could I face this woman again? How could I face anyone with the last name McClain again?

But, as I washed my hands, her moans and whimpers kept playing in my mind. Then the sight of her big, round ass jiggling popped into my head along with the sound of me sliding in and out of her. Next thing I knew, I had a hard dick and a headache.

Yeah, I truly fucked up.

Kathryn

I had spent the balance of the day thinking about the man who'd taught me a new definition of good dick.

Got. Damn.

Tommy was…indescribably good between the sheets, or rather, on my couch. Who knew that quiet giant could work a vagina like that? I mean, shit! I thought maybe he could fuck, but he could *fuck* fuck. I was actually sprung off of one dose of him, and that was just sad. And I'd been so doggone aggressive, I should've been ashamed of myself. After all, I was still legally married to Wayne's dumb ass. Which reminded me.

Me: *Hey, Wayne?*

Asshole: *Yeah, baby?*

Rolling my eyes, I texted back: *You sign those papers yet?*

Asshole: *Dinner, remember? One last dinner and I'll sign.*

Just as I was about to text back every curse word I could think of in alphabetical order, a knock sounded at my door. Looking down at the jogging pants and old t-shirt I had on, I shrugged and headed to the door, panicked when I checked the peep hole to see Tommy's chest. Yeah, he was that damn big. Everything about him was that damn big.

Whew, Lord!

To be sure it wasn't some other colossus, I yelled, "Who is it?!"

"Tommy!" he yelled back.

Cue coochie throbs. "Uh…just a minute!"

I scurried to my bedroom, threw off my clothes and threw on a tube dress, ran a comb through my bone straight hair, trotted back to the door, took a deep breath, and opened it, my mind instantly replaying the events of the previous night as I said, "Hey."

Shoving his hands into the pockets of his jeans, he stepped inside my place, letting his eyes round the living room, and I took a moment to really look at him — big solid body, full lips, sleepy almond-shaped eyes, flawless dark skin, thick, soft-looking black hair in a neat taper fade. Damn, Tommy was beautiful. How had I missed this before?

"Uh...did I interrupt something?" he asked, as his eyes landed on me, slid down my body, and back up to my face.

Oh, you like what you see, huh? You can shole get it again. "No. Wanna have a seat?"

"I'm good with standing. Uh, first of all, I had a...I enjoyed last night."

"I did, too."

"But I was wrong, *it* was wrong, and it can't happen again. I'm gonna shift the assignments so things won't be awkward between us. I just hired a guy to replace Kole — who I fired, by the way. He's got lots of experience. He used to work for a state senator. I think you'll be satisfied with him."

Well, damn. He was dismissing me? Hitting it and quitting it? Shit, was my pussy trash to him or something? I sighed and let my shoulders fall, but said, "Okay. If that's what you want," because...fuck it. I wasn't going to beg him. Not again. I'd already begged for the dick once.

But shit, it was worth it.

"It is," he affirmed.

"I understand," I lied.

"I'm glad you do. No hard feelings?"

"None at all, Tomás."

"Great."

"Wonderful."

Then we just stood there and stared at each other as if we were having a damn staring contest or something, until he finally said, "Well, I should be going."

"Okey-dokey," I said, as nonchalantly as I could manage, moving past him to open the door. When it slammed closed, I was confused until I looked up to see his big hand on it. When I tried to turn around, he pressed his body against mine, moved my hair, and licked the side of my neck. I closed my eyes and moaned, reached up and grabbed the back of his head.

"T-Tomás? I thought you didn't wanna do this ag—"

He grabbed my chin, positioning my face so that he could capture my mouth, kissing me deeply, passionately, and stealing my breath away.

I managed to turn around to fully face him and wrapped my arms around his neck, returning his kiss. His hands roved my body until he pulled my dress up and reached inside my panties, and as our tongues warred with each other, I spread my legs so that he could have his way with my yoni...and he did. He slipped his fingers inside me, moved his mouth from mine to my neck, and murmured, "Why are you doing this to me?"

On a harsh breath, I replied, "What am I doing, Tomás? I was—oh, shit! I was just gonna see you out. I...damn!"

He fell to his knees in front of me, yanked my panties down, and somehow managed to lift me from the floor, place my legs on his shoulders, and then bury his face between my thighs as I fell against the door and gripped his head while wheezing like a severe asthmatic.

He licked and sucked my clit until all I could do was close my eyes, try to remember how to breathe, and hiss through my teeth. Then static filled my brain, light flashed behind my eyelids, and I swear I could vividly hear Whitney Houston's version of *The Star-Spangled Banner* as fireworks exploded in my core.

"Shhhhhhiiiiiiiittttttt!" I howled.

Then he placed me back on the floor on wobbly legs.

"What you did," he said, finally answering my pre-orgasm question while moving us backward toward my sofa. "...is be so damn sexy. I'm tryna do the right thing, but right now? I'ma need you to ride this dick." He released me, snatched his jeans and underwear down, and as he produced a condom from somewhere and covered that dick that I was definitely down with riding, I took my dress off like my life depended on it, watched him sit his sexy, naked ass on the sofa, and then straddled him, throwing my head back as he rubbed the head of his erection against my pulsing yoni. He lined himself up with me and I sank down on him with a whimper, because the man was better than blessed!

My entire body trembled as I rode him, the feeling of him inside me so intense that I barely felt him squeezing my ass and nipping at my nipples. And when I climaxed again, I screamed like a mad woman and collapsed against his broad chest as he plowed upward until he met his own bliss.

*****

We migrated to my bedroom after he tore my ass up on my sofa, and continued what we'd started, going two more rounds before we both fell asleep. I woke up in the middle of the night, naked, sore, and alone, and although I should've been mad or insulted about him ducking out on me like that, I wasn't. Hell, I was tired, too tired to be upset. And anyway, I kind of expected it, seeing as he'd said we couldn't do what we did again, and then we did it. Repeatedly. He didn't want to upset my overprotective-ass brothers. I got it. He wasn't trying to lose his job. I got that, too. I really did. So I wasn't upset, but I also didn't want to stop doing what we were doing, because...

Shit!

Tommy was a damn pussy conqueror. I remembered wondering what in the world Bridgette was doing with him when they were together, because they seemed so mismatched. Now I knew. It was the dick, but I suppose good dick could only take things so far. As for me, I wanted to ride him to the end of the dick railway, and if we had to keep it a secret in order for him to be comfortable with it, so be it.

Staring into the darkness of my bedroom, I decided I'd let

him know that when I saw him again, and I couldn't wait to see him again.

7

Kathryn

Kim breezed into my condo, quickly handed my nephew to me, mumbled, "I gotta pee," and rushed toward my bathroom.

In response, I chuckled and kissed Little Leland's juicy cheek, and when I looked up, saw Tommy standing outside my door with a strange look on his face.

"You coming in or are you just gonna guard the hallway?" I jibed.

He turned and looked at someone, said something in a hushed voice, and then another damn titan stepped from behind him. This dude was tall and wide, wider than Tommy, and just as mean-looking.

"Ms. McClain, this is Orlando Norman, but he goes by Tree. He's the guy I was telling you about, the one who'll be protecting you — Little Leland from now on," Tommy informed me.

Oh, really now? So he was still on that bullshit? "And who are *you* protecting, Mr. Kirby?" I asked, since we were being all formal and shit.

"Mrs. Kim right now."

I glared at him, he stared at me, and Tree stared at both of us.

After a few seconds of awkward staring and glaring, Tommy finally said, "I think this will work out better."

He looked conflicted, maybe even a little sad. I, on the other hand, was pissed. We'd just been screwing a few hours earlier, and the way he wanted to handle things was like this? Okay.

Fuck it.

Again.

"Well, come on in, Tree. Let me give you the lay of the land since you'll be hanging out here a lot," I chirped. "Maybe we'll get to be friends like me and Tommy did."

I watched as Tommy clenched his jaw and narrowed his eyes at me.

Tree gave me a nod, muttered, "Yes, ma'am," and stepped into the living room, and then I slammed the door in Tommy's face, because big good dick or not, he could go straight to hell. I was done playing this see-saw game with him. Wishy-washy-scary ass...

"Kat, you might wanna steer clear of the bathroom for a while. Ended up doing more than peeing," Kim announced, once she finally made it back to my living room.

"I figured that," I replied.

"Well, I gotta get going. Me and my cousin, Zabrina, are going shopping. Hey, you wanna come to her show this Saturday? Drayveon will be there," she said, giving me a wicked grin.

I almost told her no, thought about it for a second, and asked, "You got a sitter for my baby boy?"

"Uh-huh. You coming?"

As she opened the door to reveal Tommy standing just outside it looking crazy, I said, "I think I am."

8

TOMÁS

"What the fuck?!" she shrieked, eyes wide, mouth hung open, hands on her hips. Damn, she was gorgeous in her little black dress. "Get your big M'Baku of the Jabari tribe-built ass out of this bathroom!"

"What the fuck was that shit you were doing out there on that dancefloor?!" I barked.

"Uh, I think it's called dancing?"

"You know what I'm talking about, Kathryn!"

"Oh, I'm Kathryn now and not Ms. McClain?"

"Answer my question! Why were you out there dancing and shit?!"

"Damn, I didn't know it was illegal to dance on a dancefloor!"

"You were doing that shit to get to me, weren't you? You been fucking with me all-damn-night, all up in that nigga's face! First, you talk all that shit about being friends with Tree, and now this!"

"What's wrong with me and Tree being friends? Tree is a nice guy."

"You fucking Tree?!"

"So I just go around fucking all the bodyguards, huh?"

"I didn't say that! You just...are you or not?"

"You know what? You can go to hell!"

"Kathryn, you need to stop this shit!"

"What the hell is wrong with you?! You don't even want me! You hit it and quit it! Twice! Remember?!"

"That's not what I did! I was just...I thought it was best to keep my distance from you, so I reassigned myself."

"You *thought*? Or you still *think*?"

I scrubbed my hand down my face and sighed. "All I know is that mess you pulled out there and what you said about being friends with Tree fucked with me. I don't like it. And...and I miss you. Damn, you're messing my head up."

Her eyes softened, and she opened her mouth, but for once, she didn't speak.

"Cat got your tongue, Kathryn?"

"You miss me? I miss you, too," she said softly.

"Kathryn, I...*shit*."

"You're worried about my brothers? I'm not. I don't care if they know."

I placed my hands on her bare arms, rubbed her soft warm skin. "Because you've never heard your brothers talk about killing a nigga over you, and I get it. I feel the same way about my sister. Hell, I beat the brakes off her kid's dad after he cheated on her. Plus, I'm supposed to be protecting you—"

"Not me—"

"I'm supposed to be protecting you *and* the baby, not-not having sex with you."

Her eyes dropped a second before finding mine again. "You like me, right, Tomás?"

"Mucho, baby."

She smiled at me. "Ahhh, I know what that means."

Returning her smile, I said, "Good."

"Do you like kissing me, Tomâs?"

"Sí."

"And...having sex with me?"

"Hell yeah."

"I like you, too. I like kissing you and having sex with you, and I don't wanna stop liking you or kissing you or having sex with you. So, I won't tell if you don't tell."

My eyes were all over the place. "You wanna...you wanna sneak around?"

She shrugged. "Why not? It'll be fun. I've never done anything like that before since I was with my...with Wayne forever."

All I wanted to say was yes, but I knew that was the wrong answer. I mean, it didn't feel wrong, but it couldn't be right to sneak around fucking my boss's sister, no matter how good it felt to be inside her. So I took a deep breath, exhaled, and said, "Kathryn—"

"As a matter of fact, I wanna sneak around right now."

"What? What you mean—"

I stopped talking, and my mouth dropped open as she reached under her little dress, pulled her panties down, and bent over the counter or sink or whatever, poking her round ass out and wiggling it.

I closed my eyes and groaned as I snatched my belt open, yanked my pants down, and drove into her.

She moaned, "If you're tryna hurt me or punish me...just know that I like it."

That's when I lost it, fucked her like a damn lunatic, and when we were done, I said, "Uh...I should probably leave first."

"Yeah, and I'll see you tomorrow. I'm keeping Little Leland, and *you'll* be protecting us. Right, Tomás?"

I nodded. "Right."

9

Kathryn

An hour earlier...

I waltzed into the Plush night club with my baby brother, his wife, and the rest of his entourage — including Tommy — dressed in the tightest, shortest bandage dress I could find to fit my thickness and heels that put me at Leland's height. Drayveon Walker was there, too. Not as my date, but I had my arm looped through his and was grinning at him like we were a thing. He was cute, tall, of course, and I liked him as a person. I mean, we could've easily become a thing, but Tommy had my head messed up. The furthest I could take things with Dray, as he asked me to call him, was this night at this club, a couple of dances, and maybe a grope or three. Because, see, Tomás Kirby had put his stamp on me, and his body was the only one I wanted to rub up against.

And he dumped me.

Rather unceremoniously.

Twice.

In as many days.

Because he was a damn coward.

Motherfucker...

That wasn't fair. I mean, like I said before, I got it. My brothers were his employers, my big, crazy, over-protective brothers. I swear Everett still saw me as that little five-year-old girl who cried uncontrollably when they closed the top on our daddy's casket at his funeral. The same girl who went numb when our mother died and threw everything she had into a high school romance that became a sad excuse of a marriage.

But I wasn't her. I wasn't vulnerable anymore. I could take care of myself and hold my own. I didn't need to be protected from anyone.

Anyway, I understood where Tommy was coming from. I really, really, *really* did, but I was still hurt and pissed, and I still wanted his big, sexy, Goliathan ass.

Le sigh.

"Thanks for hanging at my table tonight. I was gonna have to sit here alone," Dray said, snatching me out of my thought fog.

I smiled at him. "No problem, but you ain't gotta lie to me. I know good and well your cute, young, NBA butt wasn't gonna be sitting here alone."

He leaned back in his chair, giving me a lopsided grin. "I'm serious. Can't seem to find what I want here in St. Louis."

I pursed my lips. "You must be looking for perfection or something, because I know tons of women would want to be with you. There are a bunch of eyes on us right now."

He nodded. "Young eyes."

"Hmmm, I see now. You and Leland have the same taste in women. No wonder you two have been so buddy-buddy."

"Yeah, we do have that in common."

Adjusting in my seat, I leaned closer to him. "How old are you, Dray?"

"Twenty-two."

My eyes widened. Damn, he was too young to even grope. At least in my book, he was. I was about to reply to him when the familiar cologne hit my nose, then a baritone voice said, "Everything okay?"

My eyes climbed up Tommy's black-clad frame. "What?"

"Everything okay? You gave me the signal."

What the fuck was this nigga talking about? "Signal?"

He glanced at Dray then returned his attention to me. "So you didn't give me the signal? My bad."

Then this Mexi-negro left, and I just sat there in confusion.

"Damn, Leland's security team doesn't play. Tommy's been

staring over here since we sat down, trying to see if you were going to give the signal, I guess," Dray said.

I looked at him, my brow furrowed, but I didn't respond. Tommy had been staring at us? Was he…nah, that couldn't be it. He couldn't be jealous when *he* dumped *me*.

Could he?

Dray moved nearer to me, and said, "You're gorgeous, you know that?" His face was only inches from mine. This little boy was going to mess around and flirt up on some cougar pussy if he kept on.

I gave him my best smile. "Thank y — "

"You sure you're okay? I thought I saw you give the signal again."

No this fool wasn't back at our table.

I rolled my eyes up at him, gave him the most incredulous look I could manage, and said, "Nope. No signals given here."

Tommy nodded and left…*again.*

"Damn, how much is Leland paying him?" poor clueless Dray asked.

"Too damn much if you ask me," I muttered.

"Hey, wanna dance?" Dray requested, I think. Shit, I only half heard him, because Tommy had me completely thrown off.

Therefore my, "Sure," was reflexive. So much so, that when he stood and reached for my hand, I stared at his for a second before it clicked that I should take it and follow him out onto the dancefloor.

BJ The Chicago Kid's *Good Luv'n* was filling the club, and I smiled as Dray fell into a nice little two-step to the mid-tempo beat, joining him with a laid-back sway of my own. I closed my eyes, listening to and moving to the mellow, feel-good song, and opened them when I felt Dray's hands on my hips and his breath on my ear.

"You know I like you, right?" he asked, then moved his head so that he could look into my eyes. His eyelids hung low as he licked his thick lips.

"Because I'm old?" I joked. "Old and tall?"

He shook his head as he pulled me closer to him and led me in a dance that was way too slow for the song. "Because you are sexy as hell."

"Does Leland know how you feel?"

"Yeah."

"And he's okay with it?"

"Hell no. He threatened to, and I quote, 'Beat my ass until it roped like okra.' Never heard that shit before."

I laughed. "Leland talks like an old country man sometimes. I blame our uncle for that."

"Yeah, well anyway, Kim stepped in and stood up for me. So, now he says he'll only fuck me up if I make you shed even one tear. And by 'fuck me up,' he said he means he's gonna cut my dick off."

I threw my head back and laughed again. "Now *that* sounds like my baby brother. Hey, Dray...I think you're handsome and sweet, but—"

"I'm too young?"

"Yeah. I'm sorry."

"It's all good. You got any friends your age that won't think I'm too young?"

I rested my head on his chest as I chuckled. "I'll let you know if I run across one."

He gave me a smile and kissed my cheek. When the song ended, I excused myself to go to the restroom, almost fainted when I found that the coveted one-toilet one was vacant, and damn near jumped out of my skin when Tommy busted in there before I could lock the door behind myself.

10

Kathryn

Now...

"Leland keeping you that busy? You can't call your big brother, Kat?"

Rolling my eyes with a grin on my face, I replied, "You coulda called me. I'm the one trying to put my life back together here, *Tick*."

"Oh, so you playing dirty, calling me Tick, huh? What if I called you Kit-Kat?"

"The only person allowed to call me that is Leland and you know it."

"You and Leland...can't get along worth shit but love each other more than any of the rest of us. I swear you legit think he's your son."

"Whatever. Anyway, I know you're just calling to check on me, Daddy Everett. I'm fine."

"Wayne's bitch-ass sign the divorce papers yet?"

"Hell no." I sighed. "I don't know what I'm gonna do about that."

"Shit, put Nolan on the case."

"I could, but I wanna handle this myself."

"Big-bad Kathryn Ann, always wanna handle shit yourself. All these years, you let Wayne disrespect you when you had four brothers that would've beat that nigga's ass on command. Stop being so damn stubborn. Let Nole get someone to persuade that nigga to sign the papers."

"First of all, what man will want me after they find out that if they look at me the wrong way, my four brothers will beat

---

their ass?"

"Who tryna get with you?!" my oldest brother bellowed into the phone.

"See?"

"See what?"

"Look, I can handle Wayne."

"A'ight," Everett grumbled. "I knew better anyway. Your mean ass probably wants to beat him into signing it yourself."

"If I have to. I gotta go. Tell Jo and the kids I said hi."

"I will...mean ass."

I ended the call and resumed my prior position, snuggled up close to my giant with my head on his hard chest.

"You heard that shit, didn't you? He was ready to come through the phone at the thought of you dating someone," his rich voice rumbled.

"He was just kidding."

"Uh-huh. If you say so. But Nolan and Neil had that same energy when they called to check on you the other day."

"They're all some clowns."

"Some clowns who'll go to war over you."

"Whatever."

"Hey, why won't you let Nolan help you with the divorce?"

"Hey, why were you eavesdropping on my conversation?" I countered. "Come to think of it, you're *always* eavesdropping on my conversations."

"Because you *always* have your phone on speaker. How am I supposed to *not* listen?"

"Close your ears."

"I'm too old to be closing my damn ears."

"You're what? Two or three years younger than me? You need to respect your elders."

"I do respect you...*and* your pussy. That's what you really want me to respect, anyway. That's all you want me for."

I sat up in the bed and frowned down at him. "You sound like your feelings are hurt or something."

"They are. I'm more than my dick, Kathryn."

"I know that, Tomás."

"Then why did you attack me the second I walked in here?"

"Because I wanted that dick!"

"Exactamente."

"Oooo, you know what? I get turned on when you speak that good Spanish."

"See?"

I sighed. "You don't want me to want you, Tomás? As jealous as you are?"

"I'm not jealous, Kathryn."

"Say my name in Spanish, Mr. Fake Signal Man."

"Uh, it's...*Kathryn*."

I rolled my eyes. "Then give me a pet name in Spanish."

"Mujer que habla demasiado."

"That was an insult, wasn't it?"

"Yep."

"How you gonna be mean and jealous at the same time?"

"I said I ain't jealous."

"No? So I can date other guys, right?"

"Hell no. But that's not jealousy. That's me saving you."

"From what?"

"Wasting your time looking for what you can only get from me."

"And what's that, Tomás?"

"Satisfaction, pleasure."

"So you think you satisfy and please me?"

"I know I do. And although you're mean, vindictive, like provoking me, talk too much, use me for sex, and are bossy as hell, I wanna please you right now. You gonna let me please you?"

I smiled as he rolled me onto my back, settling between my legs. "Yes. Please, please me."

TOMÁS

"The fuck kinda question is that? I don't like this game, Kathryn," I said, rolling over in the bed to face her.

"But your Mexifrican ass is gonna play it. You accused me of using you for dick, so we're gonna play this game today. No sex. Well, no *more* sex since we already had sex today."

"Damn, I was playing with you!"

"Next time you'll know not to play with me like that."

"Ain't you supposed to be watching Little Leland while you're making up these crazy-ass games?"

"Ain't you supposed to be protecting me and Little Leland?"

"I *am* protecting y'all."

"And I *am* watching him sleep on this monitor. Now answer the question, would you rather fuck a goat or Flavor Flav?"

"Shit, I'm sorry I said what I said. I promise I'd rather be fucking you right now. Matter of fact, come here."

"No! Okay, another question. Ummm, would you rather kiss a gas station toilet seat or Joffrey from *Game of Thrones*?"

"Man, fuck Joffrey!" I yelled.

"Damn, he really is a trigger for you, huh?"

"Hell yeah. Crazy motherfucker. Him, not you. But you *are* a little crazy. When do I get to ask the questions?"

"Uh, that's not how the game works."

"How the hell does it work, then? You do all the asking and I do all the answering?"

"Yup."

"Cheating ass."

"Whatever —"

I kissed her, grabbed her ass, and said, "Enough talking. Get up here and get to work."

"Oh, so now you want the cookies, huh?"

"I always want the cookies and you know that. Come on, now. Less talking. More fucking."

She climbed on top of me, grinned down at me, and said, "Sí, señor."

11

Kathryn

"You feeling better?" my sister-in-law asked.

I took the phone from my ear and frowned at it, then replied with, "Huh?" When was I sick?

"*Are you feeling better?* When you left the club the other night, you said your stomach was bothering you, and you were walking funny."

Oh, that! In all actuality, it was my coochie that was in disrepair from the punishment Tommy put on it. Hell, I needed a cigarette and a nap after that, and I don't even smoke. "Uh, yeah. I feel much better."

"Kat?"

"Uh-huh?" I said, as Tommy stepped his sexy ass out of my bathroom, pulling his pants on.

"We're close, right? More than friends, we're sisters."

"Yeah…" I smiled at him as he bent down and kissed me, then whispered he'd call me later.

"Then you can tell me about you and Tommy messing around."

I sprung up in the bed. "What?! Girl, are you crazy?! I ain't messing—"

"Save it. I know something is going on with you two, because he looked like he was about to blow a gasket when you were dancing with Drayveon, and he stared at you all that night."

"He's a bodyguard. He was guarding me."

"Y'all were screwing in the club's bathroom, weren't you?"

"Girl, are you outta your mind?"

"I'm not going to tell Leland, if that's what you're worried about. I know what a fool he can be about you. Big South, too. I won't tell anyone, will act super surprised if — or when — ever it comes out. I'm good at keeping relationship secrets, you know?"

I held the phone for a second. Kim was trustworthy. I knew that, and shit, I needed to talk to *someone*. "Okay. I'm messing with Tommy, and he's messing with me."

"Yes! I'm so happy for you!"

"You are?"

"Yeah, girl! You deserve to be with somebody! I mean, I know how it is to be hurt and just shut down and shut everyone out, and even if this is just sex between you and Tommy, at least it's that."

"Yeah, but...never mind."

"No, what is it?"

"What if...what if it becomes more than sex? What if I like him? You think it's dumb for me to like him?"

"Why would that be dumb? What's dumb about it?"

"You know...I just got out of a long-term disaster of a relationship. Gotta be stupid to even consider another arrangement like that. Commitment, being with one somebody? That'd be crazy."

Kim sighed into the phone. "Kat, don't do that to yourself. Don't decide you don't want something before you even have it. Take it slow, get to know him better, and just let whatever is going to be...*be*. There's nothing dumb or stupid about falling in love or like, with the right man. Your ex was the wrong man. Give Tommy a chance to be the right man."

"Thank you, Kim. I swear Leland doesn't deserve you."

She laughed. "No, sis. *I* don't deserve *him*. I put him through hell, but he loves me, and I can't help but love him back."

"And I'm glad you do."

TOMÁS

"How did you find out you were diabetic?" she asked, her eyes on Little Leland in her lap. I was sitting next to her, my mouth on her neck. She smelled so good.

"Hmm, on tour with South. The schedule was hectic as hell, and it was back when he was out there with the women...before Jo. I'd be his armor during the show, follow him to some club where he'd stay until they locked the doors, have to stand guard at his hotel room door. Got little to no sleep most days, was eating on the run. It all caught up with me, and a disease that might not have shown up until I hit my forties, attacked me at a much younger age. I started feeling tired all the time, slept through my off days, got to the point where I could barely get out of bed for work. Your brother saw the difference and made me go to a doctor. Turned out my blood sugar was through the damn roof. Over five hundred. I ended up in the hospital for a week before they got it under control."

"Wow, that had to be scary as hell." Her eyes were full of concern as she looked into mine.

"It was. I'd been healthy up to that point. Shit, I'd barely ever had a cold a day in my life. Always got perfect attendance at school."

"Oh, you were one of *those* kids, huh?"

"Yep. Never missed a day and never made less than an A."

"For real?"

"Yeah! You think I'm dumb because I'm paid muscle?"

"I didn't say that. I mean, you used the word loquacious. You are obviously not dumb. I just...why *are* you a bodyguard?"

"Because it pays well."

"Well, that's an honest answer if I ever heard one."

I shrugged. "Look, I'm a big nigga and I know it, was always big for my age. Hell, I was six feet in the seventh grade. So, my options, if I wanted to make good money, were sports or medical school or something. I was never good at sports, and I was over school after high school. So I decided maybe I'd be a bodybuilder. Bulked up and got offered a job as a bouncer. That money was so good, I said fuck it and kept doing that. Moved to Miami with this chick I was seeing at the time, and that's where I met your brother. The rest is history. I'm making more money than a lot of my old friends who have master's degrees."

"Hmmm, and you like being a bodyguard?"

"I love it, especially since it led me to you."

She wore an intense expression as she asked, "You really mean that?"

"Yeah, baby. I'm glad I met your officious ass."

"Don't say words like that while my nephew is awake. I don't want him to witness me attacking you."

I raised my eyebrows. "I thought it was my Spanish that turned you on."

"That, and when you use big words, and hell, when you walk in the room. Everything about you turns me on, Tomás. *Everything.*" While her voice sounded resolute, her eyes revealed her uncertainty. She was probably afraid to be that transparent with me because of the way her husband did her. I wished I could get my hands on that motherfucker.

"I feel the same way about you, Kathryn."

She gave me one of her beautiful smiles. "I'm glad you do."

*****

"Cletus? Tomás Cletus Kirby?"

I shook my head. "Nope."

"Clevester?"

"The fuck?"

"Cleon?"

"Unh-uh."

"Cleophus?"

"Naw."

"Clejeffrey?"

"No! And what's with the *Cle* names?"

"I have this gut feeling that your middle name begins with 'Cle.'"

"Then your gut is wronger than a motherfucker. Just give up. You'll never guess it."

"Then tell me!"

I reached over to where she lay naked next to me and smacked her ass. "Never."

"You know my middle name—you know my *whole* name!"

"You have a normal middle name—Ann. Kathryn Ann McClain—"

"Don't you dare say my married name."

"Damn, you don't even want to hear it?"

"No. First of all, I never officially changed my name from McClain."

"Because you knew something wasn't right, even if you only knew it subconsciously."

"I guess so. Anyway, second of all, I don't need to be reminded of that gross error in judgement."

"But you loved him once."

"I also once believed in Santa Claus and the tooth fairy. Then I learned the truth, and I left them behind, too. I don't bring them up, don't talk about them. I erased them just like I did my ex."

"You erased all those years you were with him, too?"

"Yep."

"I don't believe that. You can't erase a part of your life that lasted that long."

"I can and I did. And...I don't want to talk about this anymore." She turned from her stomach onto her side, her back to me now.

"Why are you so damn angry all the time?" I asked.

"Because I have to be. It's called survival. Vulnerability and kindness are weaknesses I can't afford to have anymore."

"You let him change you? You let him have that kind of control over you? That's fucked up."

"It's not control, and he didn't change me. He just showed me the truth about this world, about how it'll eat you up if you let it."

I stared at her back for a moment, inexplicably turned on by her words. Then I scooted closer to her, let my hard dick rest on her thick ass, and said, "I wanna eat you up right now. You gon' let me, Kathryn?"

She rolled over, a big smile on her face as she slid down my body. "Mmmm, let me go first."

As she wrapped her lips around me, putting me in her warm mouth, I closed my eyes, and moaned, "Shit, go ahead."

12

Kathryn

Me: *Wayne, sign the damn papers. Today. Stop playing. We need to get this over with.*

Sir Little Dick: *Have dinner with me.*

I sighed as I sat in the arena next to Kim. I should've been focusing on the game, but I was tired of the loose ends dangling in my life. Me and Tommy — shit, I didn't know what we were doing, but I wanted to keep doing it. Maybe I wanted to do it forever, but as long as I was handcuffed to my fraud of a husband, that wasn't even a possibility.

Me: *OK*

Sir Little Dick: *Really?*

Me: *Sure. We can do it over Skype.*

Sir Little Dick: *No. I want us to sit down at a table in Morton's and eat our favorite meal together. In person. And after we share our favorite dessert, I want to kiss your pretty cheek and then I will sign the papers.*

Me: *Morton's in Houston? Fuck you! I'm not taking a walk down memory lane with your cheating ass! Sign the fucking papers you ass crack!*

Sir Little Dick: *I will. After we share dinner. At Morton's.*

Me: *Again, FUCK YOU!*

I blew out a sigh and slid the phone into my purse, turning my attention back to my favorite little brother as he raced down the court.

13

TOMÁS

"Has this ever happened before?" I asked, staring at her pussy.

She shook her head, reaching down and resting her hand between her open thighs. "No. Try again."

"Baby, it's not gonna let me in, and I ain't down with breaking my dick trying."

"Tommy, you can't break a dick."

"I ain't about to find out."

She sighed and closed her eyes. "Well, I guess maybe five times was enough."

"You think? This game was a crazy idea anyway." The game I was referring to was, her idea for us to have sex every time someone had sex during the *Game of Thrones* episode we were watching. I was going in for round six when her pussy locked up on me, and I don't mean that it figuratively locked up. It *literally* locked up on me, was clenched so tight, I couldn't even get a finger in it.

"So, you didn't enjoy the game, Tomáááááás?"

"I enjoyed the shit out of it. So did Mr. Kirby."

She giggled. "I still can't believe you call your peen that."

"What would you call him?"

"*Professor* Kirby, because he has taught me the true, Encyclopedia Britannica meaning of *good dick*."

Giving her a lopsided grin, I said, "Is that right?"

"As if you don't know."

I shrugged and lowered myself to kiss her. Then I left the bed, stumbling a little on my way to her bathroom.

"Your sugar low?" she asked.

"Nah, my sugar didn't do this to me. You did."

"Oh! I got your big ass weak, huh?"

"You *keep* me weak, and not just physically," I shouted from the bathroom, as I emptied my bladder, holding the wall to keep from falling. I was worn the hell out. Her pussy locking up probably saved my life, because it was so good, my stupid ass was going to keep diving in it until I passed the fuck out. "I think my dick is chafed," I added.

"For real?"

"Yeah, for real."

"Sorry. Hey, you know what I just thought about?" she asked, still in the bedroom.

"Naw, what?" I replied, as I shuffled to the sink to wash my hands.

"I've never been to your place. We've been doing this for what? Three months now? And you always come here. I don't even know what your place looks like."

"Not much to see. Barely furnished. I work too much to need anything other than a bed, and that's only when I'm not in yours."

"You got another woman or something?"

I returned to the bedroom and sat at the foot of the bed, my back to her as I gazed at the TV hanging on the wall. "Would you care if I did?"

"What?"

I turned to look at her pretty, mean, bossy ass. "Would you care?"

"Hell yeah, I'd care! I don't share my man! Not intentionally, at least."

"I'm your man?"

"Yes! Much pussy as I've been giving you. What else do you think you are?"

I shrugged. "Your side nigga, seeing as you got a whole husband in LA."

Her mouth dropped open. I'd rendered her speechless again.

"Yeah, forgot about that, huh? We're together all the time,

and I enjoy it. I enjoy *you*, but I ain't never wanted to be no one's side nigga, Kathryn."

"Where is this coming from? Since when did you start having a problem with my marital status?"

"Since three months into this thing we got going on, I find myself still a side nigga, and like I said, I ain't never wanted to be no one's side nigga." Maybe I was coming out of left field with this, but the shit was beginning to get on my nerves. I mean, how hard was it to get a divorce in this day and age? I was feeling her, *really feeling her*, like introducing her to my mom feeling her. How in the hell was I going to look my mother in the face and introduce her as my woman, knowing she was still married to another man? My mom would figure that shit out. She could always see into and through people. It was both a gift and a curse for her.

"Well, I ain't never wanted to be anyone's secret woman, but I'm going along with it because you asked me to."

"I didn't ask you to do that. You volunteered."

"I don't see your ass making any damn announcements about us! How about that, Tomás? You ready to tell my brothers about us?"

"Shit, should you be publicly dating me anyway when you're still married to that man? That can't be good for a pending divorce."

"That…that situation was never a real marriage. I told you that! He hasn't been true to his vows in years. Hell, he broke them before he took them!"

"Then finalize the damn divorce, Kathryn!"

"I'm trying to! I told you he won't sign the damn papers! I can't *make* him sign them! I can't make him do anything!"

"Nah, you ain't that passive. You get what you want, talk shit until you get your way. Hell, you even jumped on the man. You're a fucking bully. If you really wanted a divorce, you'd have one by now."

"And this is when I bully your overgrown ass out of my house. You are dismissed. *Leave.*"

"So you're putting me out for telling the truth?"

"I'm putting you out for insinuating that I still want to be married to that baby-dicked, cheating asshole!"

I sighed and shook my head as I stood and moved around the room, gathering my clothes. "If that's what you want, I'm out."

"Oh, it's definitely what I want, Mr. Kirby."

"A'ight."

A few minutes later, I was in my car, leaving the parking lot of her building.

Kathryn

He's an asshole anyway. It's not like he loves me or I love him. We were just fucking, good fucking, but we weren't in a real relationship. It was probably never going to be a real relationship anyway, because his big ass is scared of my brothers. So that makes him a chicken shit nigga. A chicken shit nigga with good dick is still a chicken shit nigga...with good dick.

Shit.

I was sitting in the back of one of Leland's rented SUVs, on my way to the airport so I could follow my brother and employer to his next game. Tree was driving me, and Tree was nice and respectful, but he wasn't Good Dick Tommy. The same Good Dick Tommy who left my condo and didn't look back, had barely spoken to me in a week although we were traveling together as a part of the same entourage. And yes, he'd switched himself out with Tree *again* as my protector.

Indecisive ass.

I didn't need that vacillation in my life anyway!

And yeah, I know I put him out, so I essentially caused this break-up, if you can call it that, but shit, did he have to just...go along with it?

"Now you sound crazy. What did you want him to do? Stay there after you told him to leave?" myself asked.

And I told myself, *"I wanted him to fight for me!"*

"Fight who? You?"

I blew out a loud breath, now frustrated with this internal conversation and angry that myself was right. I did sound crazy. Hell, maybe I *was* crazy, but who could blame me with my track record in the love department?

Love?

Was that what this was? Did I love Tomás Kirby? And if I did, did he love me back?

At that moment, as Tree glanced at me quizzically in the rearview mirror, because I was probably wearing my jumbled emotions on my face, I realized I wanted that more than anything. I wanted Tommy to love me, because I loved him. It was too soon, it didn't make sense, but I loved him.

I really did.

14

TOMÁS

Having to be around her all the time was torture for me. There wasn't a moment when I was in her presence that I didn't want to touch her, kiss her, *feel* her. Her perfume alone had me sitting there with a hard dick right at that moment. I needed to excuse myself, go to the bathroom and try to get my shit together, but I couldn't, because I missed her problematic ass. I missed her lopsided games and pissy attitude. I missed everything about her. Hell, maybe I was in love with her or something.

Naw, that couldn't be it.

"Can we talk alone? This is a private matter," she said, her eyes drifting over to me. Well, that shit stung, but I guess there wasn't an *us* anymore, so whatever. Standing from my seat on a chair in the corner of Leland McClain's huge living room, I offered, "I can leave. I need to hit the head anyway."

"A'ight, man. I'll be ready to bounce as soon as me and Kat get done talking," Leland said.

I gave him a nod, glanced at the woman who made my damn insides shift with just her smile, and left. I did go to the bathroom, then headed back, standing just outside of the living room. Out of sight, but not out of earshot.

"How many days you need off? Damn, you know shit is gonna fall apart if you don't keep it together for me. We're in the middle of negotiations for that car lot franchise I'm tryna buy." Leland was damn near whining. So she was taking some time off? I wondered what that was about.

"You don't have any meetings scheduled for the car lot deal during the time I'll be gone," Kathryn informed him.

"What about HMH films? Any meetings for that? And I got

that damn promo shoot for Spartan around that time, don't I?"

"I've taken care of all business-related issues and updated your online calendar. If there are any loose ends, I'll tie them up before I leave."

"You just gonna leave Little Leland to go run in behind that nigga, though? Shit, you're basically his second mama!"

"You know I love Little Leland, and I *am* his second mama, but I'm not leaving him to run in behind Wayne. I'm going to tie up my own loose ends with him."

"Man, you better not take that nigga back, Kat. If you do, I'ma beat his ass *and* fire you."

"Damn, really? You're threatening me about doing some shit that I would NEVER do? Really, Leland Randall?"

"You love that nigga. That's more than obvious. Why else would you put up with his worthless ass for so long, Kit-Kat? I just...I don't want you hurt no more. If he hurts you again, I'ma fucking go to jail. I'm not playing."

"I love you, too, little brother, and you have nothing to worry about. I wouldn't take Wayne back if he was the last man on Earth, and I *don't* love him. Not anymore. I need to end this marriage, and meeting him in Houston is the only way. Everything is done. All I need from him is his signature on the dotted line, and if I have to hold his damn hand and make him write his name, I will. I just wanna be free of him, once and for all."

"Aw, shit...you're gonna whoop that man's ass again, ain't you?"

"I'm not planning on it."

"Yeah, you are. Look, I'm down with you going to wrap up this divorce, but you gotta take some security with you. Tree is you and the baby's shadow, right? I'ma pay him extra to follow you to Houston. The season is over for the Cyclones, but I ain't got time to be having to fly to Houston to bail your violent ass out of jail with all this business stuff I got going on."

"You're doing the absolute most, but fine. Tree can go. He can stay at Ev's, too."

"Cool."

Before I could stop myself, I was walking back into the room, trying to figure out how to get myself on that trip with her instead of Tree, because if she was going to meet that motherfucker, I needed to be there whether she wanted me there or not.

"Hey, Tommy. Good timing. I know this is Tree's day off, but I need you to get with him, have him call Kat. He's going to Houston with her in a couple of weeks," Leland said.

"I can go. I mean, it'd be better for me to go, don't you think?" I said.

Leland shrugged. "I'm good with you going if Kat is." His phone buzzed, he checked it, and excused himself. "This is Zo Higgs, probably calling about this movie we're filming right now. Y'all two can figure this out. Tommy, just make sure whoever goes keeps her ass out of trouble."

Once he'd left the living room, Kat looked up at me and shook her head. "You don't want to go with me."

I sat down across from her, and said, "I know you think you know everything, but you don't know what I wanna do."

"Okay, why would you want to go with me? It's not like..." she glanced at the room's doorway and lowered her voice. "It's not like we're together anymore."

"*You* made that decision, not me. I'd still be with you, still be sleeping in your bed and pleasing the hell out of you, if you hadn't dismissed me."

"You hurt my feelings, and then you turned your back on me again."

"I didn't turn my back on you. I gave you the space you obviously needed to figure out what you really wanted. I already knew what I wanted, Kathryn. *You*."

"Do you...do you still want me?"

"I do, baby. So let me go with you. Let me be the one to protect you, and if that nigga gets down wrong with you for even a damn second, let me be the one to fuck him up."

She stared at me, and then gave me a smile. "I've missed you, and I'm sorry if what I said made you think that I really wanted you to leave and that I didn't want to be with you, because I do."

"So that's how you apologize to a nigga? Really, Kathryn?"

She raised her hands, palms up. "That's all I got."

Shaking my head, I said, "You are something else."

15

Kathryn

My mind was everywhere and on everything. I wasn't nervous or scared. I was…tired. Tired of being connected to Wayne, tired of my past encroaching on my present. Just fucking tired. Jesus didn't die for me to have to deal with this fool forever.

I shifted my focus from the back of the seat in front of me to Tommy right next to me in the window seat. He was staring out at the clouds, looking uncomfortable in his seat despite us being in first class.

"Did Leland pay for your ticket, too?" I asked.

Without turning to look at me, he nodded.

"You like flying?"

He shrugged. "Don't like it or dislike it. It's just a part of my job."

"I guess you've been all over the world with Ev, huh?"

He finally turned his head to look at me. "Yeah, several times over."

"I'm jealous."

"You haven't traveled much?"

"Other than between LA and Houston and now with working for Leland in St. Louis, not really. I mean, I did go on one tour with Everett, back when I was like fourteen, but then he started dating Esther and she started tagging along. I always hated her ass, so I stopped touring with him."

"Yeah, she's a piece of work. Glad I wasn't around while they were married."

"You *should* be glad. Anyway, after they split, I was too wrapped up in Wayne to follow Ev, and Wayne wasn't into traveling."

He tilted his head to the side, fixed those hypnotically lazy eyes on me. "You really loved him, didn't you?"

I dropped my eyes. "Tommy, I don't even know. More than anything, I think I just needed someone. I was young, my mom died, I'd already lost my father, and...he became a savior of sorts in my mind. I'd lost so much, I just wanted to hold onto something. I needed something that I believed wouldn't be taken away from me. He was that something."

"You sure you're ready to let him go?"

"We're getting along right now, Tomás. Don't make me say some shit you're gonna regret."

"Something *I'm* gonna regret?"

"Yes, something that'll make you think I don't wanna be with you and then you'll leave me, and this time, I'll have to kick your ass for leaving me. So there you'll be, ass kicked, because you made me say some shit I didn't mean."

"You are crazy as hell. You know that?"

"And here you are with me. What does that say about you?"

"That I like crazy women?"

I rolled my eyes.

"Look, I'm just messing with you. Shit, ain't no way you still want him and you got access to Professor Kirby. I know I done put this dick on you...*properly*."

"You think so, huh?"

"I *know* so. As a matter of fact, I bet you want some of The Professor right now."

In response, I took the cardigan that was sitting in my lap, draped it over his, glanced around the cabin, placed my hand under the sweater, and slid it into his jogging pants, playing with The Professor while Tommy softly hissed and moaned, eventually exploding in my hand.

*****

"There she is, still looking like she did when she was running around in these woods trying to keep up with her brothers!" Aunt Everlina greeted me.

I stepped into her arms, let her pull me into her warm, soft body, and replied, "Hey, Auntie." Stepping back a little, I inhaled the heavenly scent of food, and asked, "You cooked?"

"You know I did! We got pork chops, some great northern beans, cornbread, and rice and gravy."

"You didn't have to go to all that trouble for me. I could've sent Tommy out for something."

"Speaking of Tommy. Boy, you better get over here and hug me. Standing over there like you ain't family!" Aunt Ever declared.

As Tommy stepped into my aunt's arms, I let my eyes sweep over my brother's kitchen. I'd always loved this house, Everett's Houston home, but in the past, I was too preoccupied with who Wayne was texting or calling to really enjoy being here. I'd let my wayward husband ruin a lot of things for me, had sacrificed holidays with my family because he wanted to spend them with his. Had spent nights alone in bed, waiting for him to come home from wherever he was spending his time, but this house was special, and maybe with Tommy, I could create better memories here.

"Well, y'all wash your hands so we can eat. I know you got to be hungry after flying in that plane and walking through that Houston airport. I hate that damn airport. The thing probably got its own zip code! Just don't make no sense!"

I chuckled, and so did Tommy. Aunt Ever hated flying, and she made sure the world knew it.

"...yeah, you whooped that negro's whole ass, Niece! Ooowee! I ain't seen a woman beat a man's ass like that since that time your mama whooped your daddy!" Uncle Lee

Chester shouted, leaning back at the dining room table, rubbing his stomach. He'd showed up to see me — there was no such thing as making a trip back home without seeing at least all of my relatives — and when he smelled the food, he invited himself to dinner. Now, it was just me and Aunt Ever at the table, held hostage by his shenanigans. Tommy had taken his food into the living room, because that's what he usually did. He'd make sure the place was secure and then kind of blend in. I'd rarely seen him sit down and eat at the same table as Everett or Leland, and I guess he also wanted to give me time with my family. But, full disclosure? I just wanted to be with him. I really needed Wayne to get on board with this divorce, and I definitely needed to stop being so crazy with Tommy, because I wanted him in my life permanently.

"I still can't believe my mama was ever that mean, Unc," I said, shaking my head.

"Shiiidddd, Juanita Jean was a pistol and she didn't play about Randy. I never knew him to cheat on her, though, especially after she whooped his ass for giving that loose-ass, snake-hipped Fuller girl a ride home. Then she found that Fuller girl — Ruthie was her name, I think — and she dragged her ass down the road, too! Your mama wasn't nothing nice!"

"She beat my daddy like that just for giving that girl a ride home?"

"Baby, Ruthie Fuller was a hound if I ever seen one. She was giving it up outta both draw legs to anyone willing to take it. Now, I don't believe your daddy touched her, and your mama didn't believe he did, either, but there she was at home with Tick and baby twins. She whooped his ass just in case he got any ideas," Aunt Ever explained.

"Mm-hmm, and he never got no ideas. He knew Juanita Jean's big ass could do worse if she wanted to. My sister was just as mean as she was kind. And you just like her! A viper!" That was Uncle Lee.

All I could do was smile. Whether she had been mean in

her past or not, being likened to my mama in any way was nothing but a compliment. I missed that woman with my every breath.

"Kat, tell me something," Uncle Lee pulled me back into the conversation. "Did you know that boy had sugar in his tank when you married him?"

"Uh, what?" I asked, confused as hell.

"Did you know that Wayne was a lezbeen?"

"Lord Jesus. Lee, please stop," Aunt Ever said.

"Naw, now…I wanna know!"

"Are you saying that Wayne is gay, Unc?" I queried.

"Shit, ain't he? A man that pretty gots to be! Not that there's anything wrong with that. Shit, ain't my business which way that man likes his cookies baked, but I'm just wondering why you married him if you knew about it."

"Unc, he's not gay…I don't think. He always cheated on me with women."

"Sho' nuff?" Uncle Lee asked, his face all screwed up. "Umph. Well—damn! This ain't nobody but Lou's ass!" After hitting the button on his Bluetooth, he shouted, "What-up-there-now?! Huh? I know you didn't call me for this shit. Lou, I ain't had the damn remote. You always holding the thing hostage! Huh? Well, shit…if you can't find it, I guess you gon' miss *The Big Valley*…what?! Dammit, I'm on my way. You want a damn plate? Okay."

"What's done happened now?" my aunt asked.

"Lou's ass done lost the damn remote, talking 'bout she so upset about it, it feels like her damn pressure is going up. Can you fix her up a plate so I can go on home before she call me again? Gon' make me late for my card game!" Unc replied.

"I'll fix her a plate, but you don't need to take your old ass to no card game. Wasting all your damn money."

"That ain't none of yo' got-damn business, Ever!"

"Then why you bring it up?! Hell, don't get mad at me when you the one who brought it up!"

Aunt Ever and Uncle Lee stayed fussing at each other, but

they loved each other. They were who taught me and my brothers how to interact. We might fuss and roast each other, but we'd go to war for each other at the drop of a dime.

On my mama we would.

TOMÁS

"Maybe I should go sleep in the room that's usually mine when I come here with South. I mean…what if your aunt catches me in here with you?" My eyes were wide open in the dark bedroom.

"She won't. She went to her house. We got the place to ourselves."

"You sure?"

"Am I sure? Damn, are you that scared of Ev? You're bigger than him, you know? He's damn near short compared to you."

I sighed. "Right now, I'm lying in the man's house, in one of his beds, with his sister, who is naked, with my wet dick on her ass. That's bad enough, but then you have to factor in that the man is also my employer."

"Technically, isn't Leland your employer?"

"*Technically*, they both are. Look, I know you don't get it, because you ain't a black man, but there's a code, and I done shattered that motherfucker. I'm a damn turncoat!"

"You're Mexi-black, so does the code really apply to you, Tomás Clevonne Kirby?"

"I'm black. Black is black, and it ain't Clevonne."

She sighed this time. "Sometimes, I really can't stand you."

"I know. I can tell from how wet you get for me."

"You're an asshole."

"Thanks." I tightened my grip on her. "I wanna marry you one day, Kathryn."

She didn't respond, so it seemed I'd made her lose her words once again.

"You hear me?" I asked.

"Yeah...really?"

"Uh-huh, if you'll let me. Will you let me?"

"Don't you need to be in love with me to marry me, Tomás?"

"Did I say I wasn't?"

"But are you?"

"You nervous about your meeting with your husband tomorrow night?"

"Wow, you're just gonna run from that question, huh?"

"What would you say if I asked you if you were in love with me?"

"I'd say that I'm not nervous about meeting him. Anxious, but not nervous. I just want this over with. I don't want a long legal battle, or to have to spend months going back and forth with him trying to contest it. I just want him to sign the papers. Shit, I'm giving him everything except my business, and he already said he doesn't want it. What more could he want from me?"

"You. He wants you."

"No, he doesn't. He proved that already."

"How, by cheating on you? All that proved was that he wanted some extra ass. Wanting extra ass doesn't negate the fact that you want the main ass, too."

"Wow, sounds like you have first-hand experience with that."

"I do, but I grew out of it. Some men never grow out of it. I wouldn't do no shit like that now. Your ass is more than enough ass for me."

"Because you love me?"

I faked being asleep, snoring softly in her ear.

"I know you're not sleep, Tomás. You are such an asshole. I

swear!"

"You already said that."

"I knew your ass wasn't sleep."

16

Kathryn

It was early, so early the sun had barely risen as I opened the gate leading into Aunt Ever's backyard — the backyard of my childhood home. It was spring, but there was a chill in the air, and as I stepped onto the stone path, I pulled my light cardigan around me. Climbing the back steps, I smiled when I saw the kitchen door open; the only thing separating the kitchen from the outside of the house was the screen door, and without even peeking inside, I knew the kitchen was spotless. Aunt Ever was always an immaculate housekeeper as well as the best cook in the county. As my guardian after my mother passed, she didn't dote on me because I wouldn't let her, and I regretted that, because more than anything, I'd needed to be doted on.

"Good morning, y'all!" I called through the screen door to her and Uncle Lindell and my cousin, Barbie.

"Hey!" they chorused.

"Come on in and have some breakfast with us, baby," Aunt Ever offered. "We got some of that bacon with the skin on it. I know you always liked that."

"I sure do. I'm gonna spend a little time out here first, and then I'll be right in," I replied.

"All right, baby. I figured you'd eventually make your way back there. I'll have a plate ready for you," she said.

I smiled and nodded, then made my way down the steps and deeper into the yard, to the white gazebo that sat amongst rose bushes, a gift Everett had built for our mother years earlier — a Mother's Day gift. She loved this gazebo, spent hours just sitting in it, humming or singing. Mama had a beautiful voice that she didn't bother to hand down to me. Planting my butt on that same seat, I closed my eyes and sighed. My brothers liked to visit her grave to feel close to her, but I felt her spirit strongest in this place.

I sat there for a few minutes before I let my tears fall, and then I began to speak: "Mama, I just wanted to...I just wanted to let you know how much I miss you, how much I *still* miss you. It's like I miss you more with every day that passes. I miss you and I need you right now, because I have messed my life up. So much time wasted giving my love to a man who didn't know how to receive it, and now...I'm afraid to give it to one I think deserves it. I keep acting crazy with him and being mean, but I don't know any other way to be, and...I just—I need Wayne to release me so I can move on and maybe make things work with Tommy if he really wants me. I think he does, but I'm not sure. Maybe it's just about the sex with him." I sighed, cutting off my own rambling long enough to dry my face with the palm of my hand. "I just don't know. Hell, maybe I shouldn't trust my own heart anymore. It hasn't exactly been a good navigator in the past. Excuse my language, Mama. You woulda tore me up if I'd said hell when I was smaller." At that, I chuckled.

"She'd probably tear your ass up if she was here to hear you say it as an adult, even though she cussed like a sailor herself." Aunt Ever's voice startled me, and I guess it showed on my face, because she quickly said, "I'm sorry to scare you, baby, and I'm sorry I had my old ass out here eavesdropping on your conversation with your mama, but—can I sit down with you for a minute or two?"

I nodded. "Yes, ma'am."

She climbed the three short steps with a grunt and then fell onto the bench beside me, placing her hand on my thigh. "Kat, baby...I'm worried about you. Your spirit just seems so dim...until you look at that Tommy boy."

"Auntie—"

"Now, I ain't one to tell nobody's business, and I can tell

this ain't nothing y'all want spread around, but I know you, even though you never wanted me to know you like I do—"

"That's not it, Auntie. I just…I was over *everything* after Mama died. You were good to me and Leland, and we needed you, but to be honest, I was afraid to get attached to another parent. I almost felt like if I let you in, you'd be taken from me, too." I swiped at my face, and added, "Damn tears."

She reached over and patted my wet cheek. "Ain't nothing wrong with crying, baby. Ain't nothing at all wrong with that. When you sat there with a dry face at your mama's funeral, I knew you were holding it all inside. Maybe now's the time to let it out."

That's when I fell against my aunt and broke down, crying tears for my mama and my daddy and myself and the babies I so desperately wanted to have but never did. I even cried for my little brother, who I knew never got over finding our mama's body when she passed away.

Aunt Ever held me in her arms and rubbed my shoulder and kissed my forehead, and when she could tell my tears where subsiding, she said, "Baby girl, I know you been hurt, your poor heart has been dealt a lot of blows, but I want you to know something: You deserve whatever that big negro who shared your bed last night wants to give you."

My head snapped up.

"Girl, I ain't dumb. The way you look at him? That's the same way he looks at you. He's just as crazy about you as you are about him. I ain't gonna tell Tick's crazy ass, because he truly thinks he's your daddy, and he might trust Tommy with his life, but he don't trust nobody with his baby sister. You mean that much to him. You know that, don't you?"

"Yeah, I know. Tommy really doesn't want him to know about us, but I think he's going overboard with the caution."

"Kat, baby…Tommy has been working for Tick for a long time, spent a lot of time with him. Hell, he probably knows him better than Jo or you or me at this point. He knows he don't play about you or anyone else he loves. Now, Tick will get over it once he finds out, but you gotta wait until the time is right to tell him. He's still getting over what Wayne did to you and is upset that he didn't know earlier. Now's not the time. Tommy knows that much about him, too."

"I know you're right. Wish I'd had you to tell me not to fool with Wayne's ass in the first place."

"Hmm, I knew that boy wasn't shit, but I also knew you wouldn't have listened if I'd told you so. Would you?"

"No, ma'am. I thought I loved and needed him. Now I know better, and like my mama used to say, when you know better, you do better."

She turned her head, and I followed her eyes to Tommy standing in the backyard near the rear of her house, his eyes on us. "I know that's right, baby."

*****

"You're just gonna sit over there and drive in silence? You mad at me or something?" I asked, glancing over at him.

"I'm thinking," he replied, his eyes still on the road ahead of us as he navigated the heavy Houston traffic. I already wished I was back at my big brother's house, because I just knew this was going to be a disaster.

"About what?"

"You. Us."

"And?"

He didn't reply, and with a sigh, I fixed my eyes outside the passenger window.

We made it to the restaurant early, and both of us just kind of sat in silence. You could almost hear our thoughts occupying the air around us. I closed my eyes while nibbling on my index fingernail and jumped a little when I felt a hand on my thigh. Opening my eyes, I looked over at Tommy who was staring at me, then dropped my gaze to his hand as he lifted the skirt of my black maxi dress, exposing my thick thighs, massaging them while biting his bottom lip.

He moved his hand up to my yoni, and I involuntarily opened my legs for him while holding my breath. He slowly rubbed me through my panties, then pulled at them until they ripped, making me jump again. I watched him with wide eyes as he rubbed my clit, his own eyes on his work below my waist. He rubbed and massaged and squeezed it until my whole damn body seized up and I was squeaking like a chinchilla.

Once the orgasm had finished assaulting me and I'd caught my breath, I asked, "W-What was that for?"

He slid his fingers, the pussy-slickened ones, in his mouth, sucked on them for a minute, and finally said, "Just wanted to remind you of what you got before you go in there and he starts reminding you of what you had."

"Uh…all I had with him was sub-par dick and heartaches."

"Exactly. And what you got with me?"

"Shit…*everything*."

"Right."

"You tore my panties, and now I'm all sticky and shit from coming."

"More reminders."

I rolled my eyes and grabbed the door handle, but he reached over and stopped me from opening the door. "Hold up," he said. Then he walked around the rented SUV and opened it for me. I'd barely climbed out onto the parking lot when he grabbed me and kissed me deeply. "I love you," he murmured. "I love you, Kathryn."

I looked up at him, into those lazy-lidded eyes of his. "You do?"

He nodded. "Very much."

"I love you, too, Tomás."

"Good." He reached around and smacked my butt. "Now

let's go get these papers signed."

"Okay. If anything goes wrong, I'll just give you the signal."

He frowned. "What signal?"

"The fake one from the club that night you broke into the restroom on me."

"You just can't let shit go, can you?"

"Nope."

17

Kathryn

Morton's looked exactly the same inside, smelled the same, felt the same, and brought on lots of old memories, fond memories of a younger me and Wayne, but those memories weren't fond enough to erase the nights I'd cried over the man who sat across from me. As a matter of fact, being there in a place that'd once been special to us only made me feel worse about where we'd ended up as a couple, and the big man sitting at the table next to ours made the urgency of ending our marriage even more apparent.

"I can't believe you brought a bodyguard. You know I'd never put my hands on you, Kat. I'd never do anything to hurt you," Wayne said, sitting there looking like Quincy Brown—Al B. Sure's fine-ass son.

"But you *did* hurt me," I countered. "Repeatedly."

He dropped his green eyes. "I know…I meant *physically*."

"Emotional pain is just as bad as physical pain, Wayne."

"Yeah…"

The waiter arrived, and Wayne ordered the mussel appetizer and two lobster entrees for us, our regular meal, and once the waiter left, he said, "You remember the first time we came here? You'd been here with Everett and kept raving about the food, especially the mussels, and you wanted me to experience it. I drove us here in my beat-up car, and you paid for the food."

I just stared at him, because I didn't feel like helping him reminisce about a past during which I was a total and complete fool for him.

So he continued: "I was just a country boy. Countrier than you, because I didn't have a rich big brother who could expose me to stuff like this, but the thing about you was, you wanted me to experience those things. You wanted to open my world up from the second we got together. Shit, I wasn't going to go to college at all, and then you convinced me to go, helped me with the paperwork. You always had my back, always encouraged me when my businesses didn't work out. You were...you *are* too good for me and I know it. And I'm sorry, baby. I'm sorry for everything I did to you."

It's crazy how the puzzle pieces fall into place or the light bulb pops on at the strangest time. At that moment, a realization hit me, and without even meaning to, I began to speak it aloud. "I tried to change you, to build you into the type of man I wanted. I—I pushed you into doing so many things. Maybe...maybe you were just supposed to live a country life, but I dragged you to the city, to LA. Before that, I convinced you to go to college, then to become an entrepreneur, because I thought I was helping, but maybe none of that was your destiny. No wonder things were so messed up between us. I mean, it was still fucked up for you to cheat on me repeatedly, but I can see my wrong in things now...and I'm sorry."

He frowned in a confounded way. "Um...thank you for that, but you didn't make me do anything, baby. You were just looking out for me, and I love you for that."

"Uh-huh, now I'ma need you to sign the papers."

Wayne opened his mouth, probably to protest, but my phone dinged, and I held up a hand as I checked the text message.

Tomás "Good Dick" Kirby: *About time. Shit! Hurry up and get that nigga's John Handcock because I got something for your ass. I'ma put my mouth on you.*

Smiling, I replied: *Wow, you are so romantic.*

Tomás "Good Dick" Kirby: *And you know it.*

The waiter arrived with our white wine and garlic mussels along with two plates, and after Wayne thanked him, I dug in my pink satchel Coach bag and pulled out the folded papers, handing them across the table to him. "I brought my copy in case you didn't bring yours."

He took them, stared down at them, then looked up at me. "Um...Kat, I was thinking, *hoping*, we could try to work things out. I mean...I still love you."

From my right, Tommy loudly cleared his throat.

Shaking my head with my eyes fixed on my worst mistake, I stated, "That would be a firm hell-to-the-no. Not this time. I'm not taking you back this time. I am NEVER taking you back."

"But, baby—"

"Look, you fucked up by cheating on me. I fucked up by trying to mold you into something you were never meant to be, and that includes the role of my husband. We've got a lot of years behind us—some good, mostly bad—but what we had is over, done. I need you to sign those papers, Wayne."

"Kat—"

"*Now*, Wayne."

He sat there and watched me enjoy one of those mussels, then said, "I can't. I won't."

From the corner of my eye, I saw Tommy adjust in his seat.

"You *can* and you *will*," I said.

"Kat—"

"Wayne, either you are going to sign those motherfucking papers or I'm going to have your dick cut off while you're sleep and stuffed into your mouth."

He chuckled. "I know you're bad-ass Kathryn McClain— still hurts that you never took my name—but how are you going to manage that? Huh? Who do you know that can make that happen? Or are you gonna sneak into our house and do it yourself?"

"Oh, I could do it, and you know I could." I leaned forward, my eyes blazing a trail into his, and finished with, "Or I could call Nolan, have him take care of it for me."

"I'm not scared of Nolan or his supposed connections."

"Oh, really?"

He lifted an eyebrow. "Really."

When I was younger, I hated being so tall, taller than all the girls at my school and most of the boys, eventually growing taller than Nole and Neil. And I was always so thick on top of the height, so they wouldn't call me a giraffe. Rather, they teased me about being a boy pretending to be a girl, despite the fact that I'd always been pretty as hell — and I always knew it — almost as pretty as Leland. Anyway, I used to hate having long legs, but on this night, they worked to my advantage, as did the white tablecloth.

I lifted my heeled foot and found my target, Wayne's groin. In response, his eyes widened. When he abruptly tried to move his chair back, Tommy hopped up. "What's going on?" he growled, his eyes on Wayne. Tommy couldn't have known my stiletto heel was digging into Wayne's dick. It was Wayne's sudden movement that had him on high alert.

"Sh-she's got her foot on my-my dick. I-I was trying to scoot out of her reach."

"Oh, okay," Tommy said, and then this big nigga stepped behind Wayne, pushed his chair forward, and stayed behind him. "Carry on," he said to me.

So I pressed my foot harder. "You ready to sign the papers, Wayne?"

He winced and whimpered, "This is coercion and assault!" His hand moved. I guess he was thinking about touching my foot or moving it or something, but then he looked up at Tommy, whose expression was scaring even me, and said, "I-I don't have a p-p-pen."

I dug a pen out of my purse, handed it to him, and watched as he hesitantly signed the papers with a grimace on his face. He'd just handed them back to me when Tommy moved, and said, "Ms. McClain, we should probably be going. You have that other thing you don't wanna be late for, remember?"

I looked up at Tommy, perplexed as hell, but I didn't argue, because I was ready to leave anyway. So I moved my foot, watched Wayne release a breath, and stood from the table. As

Wayne stared at us, I let Tommy cup my elbow in his big hand and lead me through the restaurant's dining room.

"Thanks for having my back," I said.

"Always. It took everything in me not to flatten his ass."

"Shit, me too." As we approached our rental, I asked, "Uh…hey, what thing were you talking about that I'm gonna be late for?"

"My dick."

TOMÁS

"Tommy, this is a mansion. Your mom lives in a mansion?" she asked, as I opened the passenger door for her.

"It's just a house, baby," I said, with a shrug.

"Didn't you say you had this built for her?"

"Yeah."

"How the-fuck much is my brother paying you?!"

I chuckled as I placed my hand on the small of her back and led her to my mother's front door. "My uncle is in construction, so it didn't cost as much as you think, but your brother does pay me well. Why you think I ain't tryna get fired?"

"Shit, I get it now! But…how much did you say exactly?"

"I didn't say, slick ass, but it's six figures, and not the low six figures."

"Damn!"

I shook my head as I knocked on the heavy mahogany door of my mom's two-story, tan-bricked house.

"How many bedrooms does this thing have?" Kat asked, barely above a whisper.

"Five."

"Wow!"

I gave her another shrug. "She deserves this and more."

"She's got to deserve it if she fed and clothed your big ass."

"But you love my big ass."

"I shole do, as my Aunt Wyvetta would say."

I laughed and kissed her hand as the door swung open to reveal my tiny sister, Josefina, who yanked me into a hug while screaming my name, then pushed me away and grabbed a bewildered-looking Kat, who towered over her.

First in Spanish, then in English, she shouted, "So pretty! And tall! No wonder he's so crazy about you!"

Kat gave me a surprised look.

"I told them a little about you, baby," I said, with yet another shrug.

Josefina dragged us through the foyer into the kitchen, where my mom was up to her usual — throwing the-fuck down. She could cook her ass off whether you wanted Mexican food or soul food, because my daddy made sure she could cook what he grew up eating, too.

"Mamá! Look who's here!" Josefina yelled, making my mom snatch around from the stove and shout, "Mijo!"

A second later, she was on me, hugging me and crying with her native tongue flooding from her mouth, and Kat was smiling at us.

"Aye, you act like you haven't seen me in years, Mamá!" I said through a chuckle, as I rubbed her back. She and Josefina were both around five feet even. I got my height from my dad.

"Ees been months, mijo! Months! Ju act like ju have no Mamá!" I guess she finally remembered I was bringing a guest and spun around to face Kat. "Dios mio! My gawt! So pritty! Tomâs, ju did not lie!"

As my mother pulled her into a hug, Kat said, "Thank you."

"Uh, Kathryn, this is my mom, Sylvia Kirby. Ma, this is Kathryn McClain," I said.

Holding Kat's face in her hands, my mom gushed, "Oh, good to meetchu! Come, come! I know ju must be hungry and tired from the drive from Houston! Let's eat!"

*****

"He beat heem up! This one was always fighting—over me and Josefina...he fight all the time! Stayed in so much trouble! He almost give me a heart attack!" my mom said, in that musical way she spoke when she was her happiest.

Holding a taco in her hand—a real taco, not that fake crunchy shell shit—Kat cut her eyes at me but said to my mother, "So, he was a troublemaker? I can see that."

I rolled my eyes and took a swig of water.

"He was! But it was just because he's so protective, especially after hees father died. That's why he good at hees chob! So Big East is chor brudder? He a good man! Always been good to my Toe-mee."

Kat finished chewing her food and nodded. "Yeah, uh...my big brother is the best."

"So, Kathryn, when ju and Toe-mee give me grandbabies?"

Kat started coughing, and I said, "Ma! Stop! You need to be telling me why I had to hear about your car breaking down from Uncle Jesús?"

My mom sucked her teeth and crossed her short arms over her chest. "He should not have told ju!"

"But he did. Why didn't *you*?"

"Because ju give me enough already! This house, the furniture, money. Ju do too much, mijo. Too much."

"No such thing as too much when it comes to you and big-head Josefina."

"Shut up!" my little sister shrieked, making her two-year-old son, Alex, giggle through a mouth full of rice.

"He so hard-headed, Kathryn. I don't know what ju gonna

do with heem," my mom directed at Kat.

She shrugged, giving me a smile. "I guess I'll just have to keep on loving him."

"Awwww," my mom and sister sang.

Then my mother fixed her eyes on me. "Ju need to marry this pritty girl and give me more grandbabies, Toe-mee. I been waiting forever!"

"Uh…" was all I got out before Kat said, "We're working real hard on both."

And to that, my mom, sister, and little nephew all laughed.

And my mother announced, "Oooh, I like her, mijo!"

"Your mom and sister are so tiny and cute, like two little dolls. Skin so dark and smooth, and they are both so sweet! Your nephew? I could just eat him up! All of y'all got those damn eyes, too! All of y'all!" Kat expressed, as we began the five-hour drive back to Houston.

"What's wrong with our eyes?" I asked, keeping mine on the road.

"They're damn hypnotic. I swear you did something to me with those eyes, got me all crazy about your gigantic ass."

"So it's my eyes? All this time, I thought for sure it was my dick."

"Shiddddd, you think it ain't?"

I had to laugh at that.

"Anyway," she continued, "your family is everything, baby. Thank you for letting me meet them. Makes me feel like we're a real couple now."

"We *been* a couple, baby," I replied.

"Really? Since when?"

"Since the first time I slid inside you."

"How about when you kept dumping me?"

"Kat, just because I felt that it was wrong to be with you doesn't mean I didn't want you or need you."

"So, you haven't been with another woman since the first time we had sex?"

"Nope. And long before that."

"For some reason, I believe you."

"Because you know I'm not a liar."

"No, you're not. You're a good man, Tomás Kirby. You remind me a lot of my big brother, Ev, you know?

"That's definitely a compliment, baby."

"Hey, you called me Kat."

I frowned. "When?"

"A few seconds ago."

"Oh. Something wrong with that?"

"Yes. I like that you're the only person who calls me Kathryn. You need to keep that energy."

I chuckled and shook my head. "Yes, ma'am."

"What do you think about what your mom said about us getting married?"

"I already told you I plan on doing that if you'll let me."

"Okay, what about having kids? You want kids, Tommy?"

"I do. Always have. You?"

"Yeah. I always wanted them, too, but didn't feel right having them with Wayne."

"Good thing I'm not Wayne, huh?" I asked, as I glanced over at her.

With her eyes on the windshield, she replied, "That's a very good thing. Hey, baby?"

"Yes, with your talking ass."

"See how you act, and all I wanted to know was how your sugar was doing. You checked it before we ate, right?"

"Yeah, it's fine."

"Good. I don't need you to get weak and have a wreck or something."

"You just saw me eat. Why you think I'ma get weak?"

"Because I'm about to do something that might deplete

your blood sugar."

"Something like what?"

"This."

She reached over and unbuttoned and unzipped my jeans, and when I looked over at her, she licked her lips and gave me a wink. Shiiiiit, I knew what that meant. So I lifted my ass, let her slide my pants and underwear down, and damn near ran off the road when she leaned over the console and slid me into her mouth.

I groaned as I placed one hand on her head, keeping the other one on the steering wheel, and whimpered, "Te amo, baby. Shit...te amooooooooo!"

18

Kathryn

Professor Kirby: *What color are your panties?*

Me: *Does it matter? You don't have any respect for my panties, the way you love to rip them.*

Professor Kirby: *I'm trying to see what color I'ma get to rip tonight.*

Me: *I'm rolling my eyes internally.*

Professor Kirby: *And I'ma roll something else internally tonight. My place or yours?*

Me: *I FINALLY get to see your place? Really?*

Professor Kirby: *Yeah, because I got me a couch and more than one set of sheets now.*

Me: *Why you so damn cheap?*

Professor Kirby: *I ain't cheap. Just like to save my money.*

Me: *No, you're cheap. Remember that time I told you I wanted some Wendy's and you got me nothing but stuff off the dollar menu?*

Professor Kirby: *Remember how fast your ass ate it? And was that necklace I got you last week cheap? Spoiled ass. And do I be cheap when I be eating your pussy? Huh?*

Me: *I'm not spoiled and what does you eating my pussy have to do with money?*

Professor Kirby: *Exactly.*

I looked up to where he sat in the corner of Leland's living room looking innocent, his face still in his phone, and typed back: *You're so damn silly. I ate tuna for lunch today. You still gonna eat my pussy tonight?*

"...I think that's it? You get all that? I see you been typing in your phone nonstop since we started this meeting." That was Leland, who I hadn't paid a bit of attention to since halfway through this meeting when Tommy entered the room looking like a night of good sex and started texting me.

Professor Kirby: *Shit yeah! You know them mangoes you be eating keep that thang sweet, I'ma just put some tartar sauce on that mug and go to town! We gotta celebrate your divorce being finalized. It took long enough.*

I smiled. Once Wayne signed, it really didn't take that long since I'd filed for the divorce over a year earlier, but I got what he meant. It felt good to know that phase of my life was officially over.

I dragged my attention from my phone and my man to my brother. With wide eyes, I said, "Can you repeat the last part...for clarification? Sometimes my fingers move faster than my brain and I make mistakes."

"Damn, Kat! I hate repeating myself! Shit!" My little brother was actually pouting as his son pulled at his nose.

"First of all, you need to stop cursing around my baby. Second, what's with the attitude? You ain't paying me enough to deal with you acting all funky. Kim on her period or something?"

"Naw, she got a stomach bug. Won't let me near her because she's afraid she's gonna give it to me and Little Man."

"Well, I'm taking him home with me tonight, before y'all infect him, and you'll just have to use your hands like you did that time I caught you when you were like twelve."

Tommy snickered softly, and Leland shot him a look. "I oughta fire both of you motherfuckers."

"But you won't," I countered. "You ain't gonna do shit, Leland Randall. Give me my baby and go take a cold shower. Just text me everything we talked about today so I can do my job."

"Man, whatever."

TOMÁS

"So this is where the magic happens, where you wine and dine and screw your women, huh?" Kat said, as she took in my small, mid-town apartment. It was just over five hundred square feet, and the only furniture present was a couch, a coffee table, and a bed. That was it. The walls were bare, and there was only bottled water and a few take-out containers in the refrigerator.

"Who told you about my other women?" I asked, as I leaned against the front door, my eyes glued to this woman who'd turned my whole world upside down.

"Keep playing," she said, as she left the almost nonexistent living room, moving through the bedroom to the bathroom. I stood in the doorway and watched her search the medicine cabinet.

"What you looking for?"

"Ho' evidence."

I chuckled as I moved behind her, wrapped an arm around her waist, and kissed her neck. "Why are you like this?"

"Like what?" she asked, as she relaxed against me, closing her eyes.

I moved my hand up to her breast and squeezed. "Suspicious, when you know you got me sprung. Can't no other woman do shit for me, Kathryn, and you know it."

She spun around, backing me out of the bathroom to the bed, where she pushed me until I was sitting on it. "I wanna try out your bed, make sure the mattress is firm and not weak from you cheating on me."

As she undressed me, I grinned. "I love your crazy ass. You know that?"

Straddling me with her face hovering over mine, she replied, "You better."

"I love you so much, I would walk naked in the snow just to kiss your lips," I mumbled, as I collapsed onto her back. She was so damn soft, always smelled so good.

"I love you so much, I can't imagine *not* loving you," she said, making my heart swell up in my chest.

"Kat?"

"Yeah?"

"Why'd you give me a chance?"

She moved to turn over onto her back, and I let her, settling between her legs. The heat of her pussy had me hard again in seconds, so shit, I went back to work.

Her eyes were wide as she gasped, and said, "Oooh, Damn! Um, what d-do you mean? W-why wouldn't I give you a ch-ch-chaaaaaance?"

I closed my eyes and sucked in a breath as I slid in and out of her. "Damn, this some good pussy! Um, I'm a bodyguard. I work for your brother. I ain't exactly a catch for a woman like you."

She threw her head back, and screamed, "Shit! What kind of woman—oh! I can't talk no moooooore!"

I'd emptied inside her and had rolled onto my back and pulled her to me, when she softly said, "What kind of woman do you think I am?"

I released a breath and rubbed her arm. "Loyal, smart, successful, gorgeous. You got everything going for you, could have any man you want."

"Well, thank you for seeing me that way. Um, I gave you a chance because you're handsome and intelligent, and beneath that intimidating frown you love to wear, you're kind. More than anything, I need kindness. You're caring and self-sacrificing, a natural-born protector. Whether you were a garbage man or a bodyguard, you're exactly what I need. And shit, you make more money than I do off my business and working for Leland's cheap ass combined."

I chuckled and kissed her forehead. "Don't you make like eighty-k? That's not cheap, it's just that my job involves a lot more danger. I gotta be willing to take a bullet for your brother."

"Aw, hell naw! I love him, but bump that!"

I threw my head back and laughed.

"What about you, Tomás? What made you want me?"

"I ever tell you that the way you say my name turns me on?"

"Every day."

"Just making sure."

"Answer the question, Afri-Mex."

"Hmm, everything I just said, plus your slick mouth." She laughed. "Wow."

"You know it's true. Anyway, more than anything, I admire your love for Little Leland. That boy has his own crib, high chair, and everything at your place. If you could be that devoted to your nephew, I know you'd make a good mother. You remind me of my mom in that way. Loving. protective, only with that damn mouth she doesn't have."

"You talking shit, but you love what this mouth can do to you."

"I sure in the hell do. Hey, I'm gonna talk to South, tell him about us."

"You are? When?" she squeaked.

"When we go to LA with Leland in a few days for South's surprise announcement thing."

"You sure? I mean, you don't have to if you're not ready."

"I love you, I'm not gonna stop loving you, and I don't wanna hide it anymore. Shit, it's been what? Six or seven months of hiding something that shouldn't be hidden? It's time for us to let the world know."

"What are you gonna do if he fires you or wants to fight you?"

"I got plenty of money saved up, and I been thinking about starting my own firm. You know, a bodyguard staffing company. I've been doing this long enough to know how to make it work. And if he tries to fight me, I won't engage. I won't even entertain it. Look, I love you, and I'm going to marry you, no matter how anyone feels about it."

"God knows I love you, too, and I will marry your ass in a heartbeat."

19

TOMÁS

I moved my hand from her head to my chest, where my heart was racing out of control, put the SUV in park, and relaxed my ass, which I'd been clenching the whole drive there.

"Is it safe for me to sit up now?" she asked.

Blowing out a breath, I looked around to see that Leland, Kim, and Tree had already gone inside South's house, and nodded. "Y-yeah, baby."

She lifted her head from my lap and grinned at me while swiping at her mouth. "You good?"

I shook my head. "Hell no. You're gonna kill me if you keep doing shit like that. Next time, your ass is staying in the backseat. Gimme a piece of candy. I think my damn sugar is low."

Alarm shadowed her pretty face as she grabbed her purse from the backseat and dug inside it. "See, and you thought I was doing too much when I started keeping this candy in my purse for you. When's the last time you ate? I told your ass you don't eat enough! I swear to God if you go into a damn coma and die, I'ma beat the shit outta your fucking corpse!"

Taking the pack of Smarties she handed me, I said, "What kind of threat is that?"

"It ain't a threat! It's a damn promise! Your ass better not die on me. I'm fucking pregnant!" Her voice wavered, and I was caught between the fact that her mean ass was about to cry and what she'd just said.

I poured the whole little pack of Smarties in my mouth, and garbled, "You're what? What did you just say you were?"

She poked her lips out and stared into my eyes. "I'm pregnant, and you better not ask if it's yours. If you do,

I'ma—"

"Beat my ass?"

"Yep."

"Why would I ask some stupid shit like that, Kathryn? I know you. You're loyal, you're good—mean as hell—but good. You're not a cheater, and anyway, whose dick is better than mine?"

"You know, you're always so quiet on the job, no one would believe how much shit you can talk."

"So I'm talking shit?"

"Are you happy? About the baby, I mean?"

I gave her a slow smile and then leaned in to kiss her. "I'm fucking ecstatic, baby. Just wondering how...or when?"

"I think it happened in Texas, but who knows? I told you I stopped taking the pill after I left Wayne, and you and I have been pretty loose about protection for a while now."

She was right. I messed around and didn't have a condom the last few times we had sex when we were in Texas, and we kind of said fuck it after that. It wasn't very responsible, but at least we knew each other's status, had shared test results. She'd made sure of that, and I couldn't blame her. Besides, I wasn't mad at the outcome. I wanted kids, and I wanted them with Kat. It was just happening sooner than I'd planned. Although, this really gave South a good reason to want to kill me.

"Yeah, true," I replied.

"So...you're okay with it?" she asked softly, her eyes searching mine.

"Did you think I wouldn't be, baby? I love you. This is what I want—a family with you. So I'm glad I was already planning to tell South about us. The timing is definitely right."

She smiled widely, leaned in and kissed me, then said, "I'm excited about it, about the baby and our future. This is all I've ever wanted, too."

"Then I'm glad I was the one to give it to you."

"You're the one, period, Tommy. You really are."

Kathryn

After we finally walked into my oldest brother's estate—because it didn't seem right to call it a house—the usual ensued. My brothers roasted each other, with Nolan being the focal point. His lethal-but-nerdy ass loved him some Bridgette, and that was a beautiful thing. I liked her and could easily see that she was a better match for Nolan than my Tommy. Tommy even said he knew that when they were together, that he liked her but knew they wouldn't work because they wanted different things in life. Like Nolan, she was career-driven, and Tommy was all about family, especially building his own. And now, we were going to have one.

I had to fight hard not to rub my belly or stare at Tommy as he stood across the living room from me in stealth bodyguard mode. I loved the shit out of him. Didn't see that coming before I got to know him, but now? I couldn't see my life going in any other direction.

Anyway, this little get-together turned out to be a listening party for Everett's and Jo's surprise new EP, a smoking hot set of songs that made me want to re-enact what I did to Tommy on the way there. He tried to act like it was too much, but he loved it, and it primed him up to return the favor when we got back to Kim's and Leland's house. Since he was going to tell Everett about us and I had decided I'd be the one to tell Leland after that, then shit, at least we wouldn't have to sneak around anymore.

As I was saying, the album was fire! Everybody was raving about *Panty Gag*, and it was definitely one of the hottest songs on the album, but my favorite was another bop titled, *Evil Jo*. Man, Everett showed his ass on that one! Talking about, *"Mean as hell, short little firecracker. Threw that shit at me, had me tryna track her. She spoke her mind, said what she said. Showed me who was boss, made her throne my bed."*

Daaaaaamn! Jo got it like that?!

I knew my brother was all in when it came to her, but wow!

Halfway through the second playing of the EP, all I could think about was wrapping my legs around Tommy's waist and screwing him into a blood sugar of seventy-five. So I stared at him until I caught his eye, then lifted a brow and shifted my eyes to the door before making my way through my dancing family, out the room, and down the hall, where I waited, hoping he wouldn't be too scared to follow me.

He wasn't, and as soon as he made it to me with bemusement in his eyes, I grabbed him, kissing him like I hadn't kissed him in forever, pushing him against the wall and grabbing his crotch. He spun me around, pinning me to the wall, and I wrapped my legs around him as we continued to kiss. When he snatched his mouth away from me, I groaned.

"Waldo and Enrique."

"Huh?"

"My middle names are Waldo and Enrique."

"It is? They are? Why? I mean, what? You have two?"

"My mom is Mexican, so yeah."

"Oh…I like Enrique, and Waldo is…"

"Bad, I know. Look, I'm telling you this because you should know my full name if you're going to marry me."

The next thing I knew, he'd dug a gorgeous—and definitely not cheap—ring from the pocket of his jeans, and all I could do was gasp.

"Been carrying this around for weeks, making myself not ask you before I told South about us, but this seems like the right time. I'm not asking because you're pregnant or because you sucked my soul out of my body on the way here. I'm asking you, officially asking you to marry me, because I love you. I'll always love you, and I want to be the one who takes care of your heart from now on. Will you marry me, Kathryn Ann McClain?"

"Hell-motherfucking-got-damn-yes!" I said, watching him

slide the ring onto my finger, and then I did my very best to suck his heart out of his body through his mouth. A few seconds later, I took my mouth from his, and added, "I'm about to be Mrs. Kirby up in this piece!"

"I'm glad I don't have to fuss your ass into taking my name."

"Naw, baby. I'd be honored to take your name. And you know what? It's a good thing I got more candy in my purse, because I'm about to deplete every grain of sugar in your fine-ass body."

He grinned and kissed me. Then I heard a voice that undoubtedly belonged to Leland yell, "What the fuck?'"

The whole damn family ran into the hallway at the sound of Leland's voice like it was a church bell or something. Everett lost it, accused Tommy of fucking me in his house, and while that *was* my intention, I wasn't going to let him attack the man who made me believe I deserved all the good love he'd been giving me. So I put both him and Leland's raging asses in their place, told them Tommy was my man, that I was carrying his baby, and that we were in love and getting married. I'd made the announcement instead of Tommy, but I don't think he minded. Shit, truth be told, he looked relieved.

In the midst of that chaos, Nolan asked Bridgette for her hand in marriage. I mean, this was crazy! Everett and Neil and Jo—hell, all of us—were shocked. I mean, I knew Bridgette and Nolan had been going strong—and thank God, because if he'd brought another one of those Polish blonds around me, I was going to stage an intervention for his ass—but *getting married* strong? I wasn't expecting that.

Bridgette said yes, and the next thing I knew, Tree's mammoth ass was offering to marry them because he was an ordained minister, and then Tommy chimed in asking him to marry us. We were all to get our marriage licenses the next day and have Tree sign them. A few minutes later, I was in the kitchen trying to calm my daddy-brother, Everett, down.

"Don't be mad at Tommy. He didn't plan any of this. Neither of us did. It just happened," I said softly.

Everett shook his head. "I never liked Wayne. I never thought he was good enough for you, and I could still kick my own ass for not putting a stop to that wedding. Now here I am again, about to watch you do some shit you shouldn't be doing."

"First of all, do you really think you could've stopped me from marrying Wayne? You think anyone could've?"

"Hell no, with your hard-headed ass. Mama always said you'd go left even if left told you to go right."

"*Exactly*. And you know Tommy, have known him longer than I have. You trust him with your life, your wife's life, your kids' lives, Leland's life, but you don't trust him with mine?"

"I trust him with your life, but I don't trust *anyone* with your heart, Kat."

"From what you know of Tommy, do you really think he'd hurt me?"

He sighed. "No—I don't know."

"Okay, do you trust me to have learned enough from my past with Wayne to be able to make better decisions now?"

"Yeah, but…it's my job to worry about you, Kat. You're my baby sister. My *only* baby sister."

"But I'm not a baby anymore. I'm grown and I'm letting you off the hook. Wayne was *my* fuck-up. If things don't work out with me and Tommy, that'll be *my* fuck-up, too, but I have to try, because I love him. I really do."

"And he loves you?"

"More than Wayne ever did."

Everett twisted his mouth and blew out a breath. "Fine. I won't kill him. You look happy, so I guess I'll give him a stay of execution, but if he fucks up—"

"Yeah, yeah, yeah, and be nice to him. More than anything,

he was concerned about betraying your trust by being with me."

"Shit, he did!"

"Ev! Come on! He respects you more than you'll ever know."

"Fine! I won't curse him out either. Shit."

I stood from the kitchen table and kissed his cheek. "Now come watch me get married...again."

In response, he groaned.

TOMÁS

"So, I don't have my little book with me that tells me exactly what to say when officiating a wedding, but I Googled it and found an abridged version, if that's okay," Tree said, holding up his phone. We were all in South's living room, where our little impromptu ceremony was being held.

"Shit, works for me. Let's do this!" Bridgette said.

"Hell, yeah! I'm ready!" Kat agreed.

Nolan and I just looked at each other and shrugged.

"Okay, here we go. Dearly beloved, we are gathered here today to join these men and these women in Holy Matrimony. Is there anyone who objects to either of these unions?"

I swear, everyone's head snapped in South's direction, and in response, he muttered, "I'm good. Carry on," then added, "Got damn," under his breath.

Tree tapped on his phone, paused for a minute, then looked up at us. "Screen went blank. Anyway, Tommy —"

"Tomás," Kat interrupted him.

Everyone in the room, except South, who signed my checks,

yelled, "Tomás?!" Hell, Bridgette didn't even know my government name.

"Yes, *Tomás*," Kat confirmed. "Please continue, Tree."

"Um, okay…Tomás, do you take Kat to—"

"Kathryn," I corrected him.

"Do you take *Kathryn* to be your wife?"

"Absolutely."

"And Kathryn, do you take Tomás to be your husband?"

"Definitely."

As Tree did the vows with Nolan and Bridgette, I stared down at the beautiful woman who was carrying my child, my first son or daughter, and my mind traveled into the future, to us as a family, a little brown baby in my arms, Kat in my bed every night, and me loving her even more than I did at that moment, if that was possible, and when he pronounced us husbands and wives, I kissed her like I'd never kissed her before. In response, she reached up and wiped the eye leakage off my cheeks.

Kathryn

"Congratulations, new sis-in-law!" I gushed, pulling Bridgette into a hug.

"Congratulations! I'm so happy for you and Tommy! He really is a great guy," she replied.

"He sure is, and thank you for not falling in love with him and for y'all breaking up and stuff."

She laughed. "Um, you're welcome? Look, it's obvious seeing you two together that you were made for each other, so I'm glad you found each other."

"I can see the same thing in you and Nole. I know he's gonna take good care of you."

She gazed over at my brother, who I used to call Twin One when I was little, and said, "Hell, he already is. He's better to me than I am to my damn self."

"Hmm, I know the feeling."

Kim snatched me into a hug and away from Bridgette. "I'm so happy for you, sis! You're gonna be a great mother, but Little Leland is going to be jealous!"

"I don't know what for. He still is and always will be my baby. Ain't nothing changed!"

And that's how the rest of the evening went, with my siblings and their wives and even Jo's and Bridgette's friend, Sage, hugging and congratulating us. Everett hugged me, congratulated me, and rolled his eyes at Tommy, but I knew he'd eventually come around. Shit, he was going to have to, because I wasn't letting Tommy's big ass go for nobody.

Later that night, when we checked into a suite at the Sable Inn, I loved on that man, my new and last husband, like there was no tomorrow. Even made his sugar drop again.

Now *that's* love.

20

TOMÁS

It was so damn quiet in that room; the shit was unnerving. There the three of us sat in the huge living room, three giants eyeing each other. Well, *they* were eying *me*. I couldn't seem to focus on anything but the floor. It wasn't that I was ashamed of the choices I'd made. I didn't regret anything that had happened, but I felt...I don't know. Conflicted? I was conflicted about how the recent events of my life had unfolded, I guess. Everything was all out of sequence, but I suppose that's how destiny works.

Clearing my throat, I scooted to the edge of the chair I sat on and lifted my eyes, looking from one man to the other. "Uh, I know I owe you both an apology—"

"Damn straight you do!" South interrupted me.

"Boss Man...I know you're pissed," I continued. "You got every right to be. You sent me to St. Louis to protect Leland and his family, and I ended up with Kathryn. I don't regret that, because she's the best thing that has ever happened to me, but I realize it was unprofessional and against code as a black man."

"Man..." Leland said, shaking his head.

"And if y'all wanna fire me, I understand."

"Nigga, how the fuck can I fire you and you got a baby on the way with my damn sister? Huh?" South asked.

I frowned. "Uh...okay? I appreciate that?"

"You should," South said.

"Uh...Boss Man Number Two," I addressed Leland. "I know you trusted me to protect Kathryn, and I—"

"I should cut your dick off. If you weren't so damn big, I would," Leland informed me.

"Well, it ain't like I'd just *let* you cut my shit off..." I muttered.

"What?!" Leland yelled.

"Look, man...I know y'all mad, but I ain't finna let you cut my shit off. That just ain't gonna happen."

South and Leland glared at me. I glared back, because shit, I outsized both of them.

South broke character first, bursting into laughter. Leland soon followed suit, and I just sat there in South's living room, baffled as hell.

"Man, look...I was pissed at first, but I've had time to think and shit now, and to be honest, I'm glad you and Kat are together. You seem to be making her crazy ass happy, and if I don't know anything else, I know you're a stand-up motherfucker, so...congratulations. For real," South said.

"Uh, seriously?" I asked.

"Yeah! How long you been working for me, protecting me, having my back? Ten, eleven years? In all the ways that matter, you're my brother just like Leland and Nole and Neil. Loyal as fuck. You ain't never been reckless or unprofessional...*until now*. So I know this is real. I can look at your big ass and tell you're all in love and shit, so I got y'all's back. Just don't tell Kat. I don't need my baby sister thinking I done went soft."

"Me, too. You definitely have my support if you're willing to deal with Kit-Kat's bossy ass," Leland chimed in.

I laughed. "Yeah...your sister is a handful."

"Shiiiit, who you telling? And since Wayne's ass hurt her, she ain't down with the shits. And she got a mean right hook, too. So...be careful," Leland said.

"For real, though," South agreed.

"Yeah, I know. She's lethal," I replied, with a grin. "I actually love all that about her."

"I bet you do," South said. "So anyway, just take care of her. Do not hurt my sister, man. I mean it."

"Yeah, you might be big as hell, but don't think you can't

get fucked up. She's got four brothers, not to mention all of Nolan's connections. We'll kill your ass and they'll never find your body. Real talk," was Leland's warning.

"Understood," I said.

"Good. Can't do a toast or nothing since your big ass don't really like alcohol. Want some juice?" South asked.

"Water," I replied.

So over glasses of water, we talked about my future as Leland's employee rather than South's, since I obviously wasn't moving back to Cali, and my dream of starting my own firm. When I left to join my wife of two days in our honeymoon suite, I had a new boss and a wedding gift of a check from South, money he gave me to start my business.

Kathryn

"...and make sure ju listen to a lot of music, mija, so the baby won't be deaf," my mother-in-law instructed me.

"Yes, ma'am," I said into the phone.

"Oh! And don't eat too much cheese. He have cradle cap if ju do!"

"Mama Sylvia, you keep saying he, and we don't even know the sex yet."

"I do know! Toe-mee say ju butt getting bigger. Eessa boy!"

I had her on speaker, so he'd heard her. Cutting my eyes at him, I said, "He told you that, Mama Sylvia?"

"Sí! Sí!"

Tommy gave me a lopsided grin and shrugged. "Mamá, Kathryn's gotta go. We need to finish looking at this house," he said.

"Okay! Send me pictures of it if ju decide to buy it, mijo!"

"Yes, ma'am," Tommy answered.

After I'd ended the call, he said, "Sorry about that. She really believes all that old wives' stuff."

I shook my head. "No, it's okay. I love it. I'm from the country, so I've heard it all anyway, but I love having a mother who shares that stuff with me. I love having a mother again, *period*. Been a long time since I had one, you know?"

He snaked his arm around my waist and kissed my cheek. "Yeah, I know. So what do you think? You like this one? I know you hated how small the kitchen in the last house we looked at was, even though your ass doesn't cook."

I rolled my eyes. "Whatever, *Toe-mee*. Yes, I love this one. This place is huge, got a nice back yard, and it's close to Leland's and Kim's house. But...the price? Seems steep."

"I know, but I think they'll take a little less. I plan on doing some haggling, but either way, if this is what you want, I'ma make it happen."

"It is, and I can help with the house note, remember?"

"Kathryn—"

"Shut up. I'm helping, and if you stop fighting me on it, I might deplete your blood sugar tonight."

"For real?"

"Mm-hmmmmmm. When I get done with you, you're gonna need a whole bag of Smarties."

"Shiidddd, fight's over. You win."

21

Kathryn

"You really gonna just sit there and watch TV while I do all the work? Really, baby?" Tommy asked, as he screwed something onto our baby's crib.

"Uh, I'm the one who's pregnant. I *am* working and don't you forget it. Damn, now I gotta rewind this episode, fooling with your ass."

"You and got-damn *Game of Thrones*..."

"Like you ain't watching these episodes for the third time, too."

"I ain't say all that. You know I love them fly-ass dragons."

"That's what I'm saying."

A phone buzzed, and Tommy said, "That's yours. Mine is in our bedroom."

I sat up from where I'd been lying on the sofa and grabbed my phone from the end table, popped a gummy bear in my mouth, and had to fight not to roll my eyes when I read the text from Wayne's bitch ass: *I heard you got married to that bodyguard. Wow. A bodyguard? Really, Kat?*

Me: *Correction: I married a bodyguard with a big dick. It's huge. I mean, it's gigantic. Biggest dick I've ever seen. It be choking the shit out of me.*

Before he could respond, I blocked him, something I should've done long ago but forgot to.

"Who was that texting you?" Tommy asked, without looking up at me.

"Wrong number," I hummed in response. I didn't have time for him to hop on a plane just to get arrested for kicking Wayne's worthless ass, so I deleted the entire text conversation.

In the middle of me doing that, my phone began to buzz with a call. I answered it, putting it on speaker. "Hey, Auntie."

"Hey, baby! How you feeling?" Aunt Ever's voice filled our living room.

"Good."

"That baby still kicking?"

"When he wants to. He's kinda lazy like his daddy."

Tommy shook his head, still concentrating on putting our baby's bed together.

"Girl, you need to stop. Anybody who followed Tick around the world like that husband of yours did ain't a bit lazy," Aunt Ever said.

"Thanks for having my back, Ms. Ever," Tommy interjected.

"If you don't stop that Ms. Ever stuff and call me auntie, I'ma whoop you!"

Tommy chuckled. "Yes, ma'am…Auntie."

"You liking the new house, Kat? Those pictures you sent to Barbie's phone were so pretty! You know I can't figure out how to pull no pictures up on my own phone."

"That's 'cause your big ass is old!" I heard Uncle Lee Chester yell in the background.

"Lee, shut your black ass up!" Aunt Ever countered.

Through a giggle, I said, "Yes, I love our house, Auntie, and tell Uncle Lee I said hey."

"Here, you can tell him yourself."

A few seconds later, I heard, "Niece!"

"Heeeey, Unc. What you up to other than giving Aunt Ever hell?"

"Over here picking up a sweet potato pie Ever made for Lou's crazy ass. Hey, I'm glad I'm getting to talk to you. I wanted to tell you something."

"Okay. What's up?" I asked.

"Since you pregnant by that big-ass Tommy, you think you need to get one of them sectionals?"

"Huh? We already got a real nice sofa, Unc."

"Naw, a sectional! You know what I'm talking about. When they cut the baby out of you!"

"A C-section? Is that what you're talking about, Unc?"

"Shit, that's what I said! A sectional! You know…my boy, Lunch Meat, was so big, they had to do a sectional on Lou. Ask your doctor about it. You don't want that baby to wreck your shop, if you know what I mean. That baby be done ripped you from the rooter to the tooter. Won't be nothing left down there but memories and wishes."

"Okay, I got it, Unc. Uh…thanks for the advice."

"No problem, Niece! Now you take care, and tell your husband I said hey."

"I will."

After ending the call, I looked up to see Tommy crying laughing, and to that I said, "Sometimes I can't stand your ass. Over there laughing at my damn uncle."

He shook his head and wiped his eyes. "Naw, baby. I love your uncle."

"Mm-hmm."

TOMÁS

"Baby, you okay?"

I nodded as I stared down at my boy. He was big, filled-out, and beautiful. I was holding my greatest dream come true in my arms, and as I bent over and kissed his forehead, I wasn't ashamed of the tears that rolled down my cheeks.

"He's everything, isn't he?" Kat asked. Her entire family plus my mom, sister, and uncle were in the waiting room anticipating meeting our boy, but right at that moment, it was just us three. The Kirbys, having some alone time in that St. Louis hospital room.

"He's perfect. Just like you."

She smiled. "He reminds me of my daddy. Not necessarily his face, but his spirit. He seems so calm."

"Good thing we named him Randall then, huh?"

"Yeah...Randall Walter. Named after his two granddaddies."

I kissed my boy again, then stood from the chair next to Kat's bed, leaned over, and kissed her. "Thank you, Mrs. Kirby."

She gave me a smile, dropped her eyes to Little Randy, and said, "Thank *you*, Tomás."

Epilogue

Kathryn

Three years later...

"You're getting too big for me to carry you around, you know that?"

Little Randy just giggled as he clamped his long legs around me and clutched the collar of my shirt.

"Okay, you ready to wake Daddy up? Huh?" I asked, as I set him on the floor of our bedroom.

Randy nodded.

"Remember what to say?"

He nodded again.

"All right. Here we go."

He looked up at me with those sleepy eyes his father gave to him and I nodded, encouraging him.

With a grin on his face, he climbed onto our bed and jumped on Tommy's body, yelling, "Wake up, Daddy!" over and over again.

Tommy kept lying there pretending to be sleep, but I could see the smile playing at the corners of his mouth.

"Get up, Daddy! I got summin' to tell you!"

Tommy flipped over and grabbed Randy, tickling him. "Is that right?!" he growled.

Through a burst of giggles, Randy managed to say, "Yessss!"

"Well, what you got to tell me, little boy, huh?"

"We're having a baby! It's in mommy's belly!"

Tommy looked up at me, his mouth hanging open, and said, "What?"

I nodded in response, and Tommy hopped up from the bed, scooped Randy up, and rushed to me, pulling me into a kiss as our son wrapped his arms around both our necks.

Laughing, I asked, "Does this mean you're happy?"

"This means I'm *very* happy. I love you so much."

"I love you, too. And I think we should name it Waldo if it's a boy."

"*Hell* no!"

A southern girl at heart, Alexandria House has an affinity for a good banana pudding, Neo Soul music, and tall black men in suits. When this fashionista is not shopping, she's writing steamy stories about real black love.

Connect with Alexandria!
Email: **msalexhouse@gmail.com**
Website: http://www.msalexhouse.com/
Newsletter: http://eepurl.com/cOUVg5
Blog: http://msalexhouse.blogspot.com/
Facebook: Alexandria House
Instagram: @msalexhouse
Twitter: @mzalexhouse

Also by Alexandria House:

The McClain Brothers Series:
Let Me Love You
Let Me Hold You
Let Me Show You
Let Me Free You
Let Me Please You (A McClain Family Novella)

The Strickland Sisters Series:
Stay with Me
Believe in Me
Be with Me

The Love After Series:
Higher Love
Made to Love
Real Love

Short Stories:
Merry Christmas, Baby
Baby, Be Mine
Always My Baby

Text alexhouse to 555888 to be notified of new releases!

Printed in the USA
CPSIA information can be obtained
at www.ICGtesting.com
CBHW081554301124
18254CB00058B/881